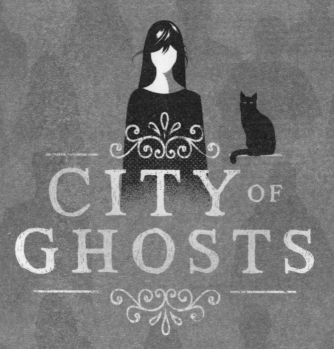

CITY OF GHOSTS

CITY OF GHOSTS

VICTORIA SCHWAB

SCHOLASTIC

Scholastic Children's Books
An imprint of Scholastic Ltd
Euston House, 24 Eversholt Street, London, NW1 1DB, UK
Registered office: Westfield Road, Southam, Warwickshire, CV47 0RA
SCHOLASTIC and associated logos are trademarks and/or
registered trademarks of Scholastic Inc.

First published in the US by Scholastic Inc, 2018
First published in the UK by Scholastic Ltd, 2018

This edition especially published for BookTrust in 2020

ISBN 978 0702 30621 1

A CIP catalogue record for this book
is available from the British Library.

Printed by CPI Group (UK) Ltd, Croydon, CR0 4YY
Papers used by Scholastic Children's Books are made
from wood grown in sustainable forests.

3 5 7 9 10 8 6 4 2

www.scholastic.co.uk

TO THE CITY
WHERE I KEEP MY BONES

"TO DIE WILL BE AN AWFULLY BIG
ADVENTURE."

~J. M. Barrie, *Peter Pan*

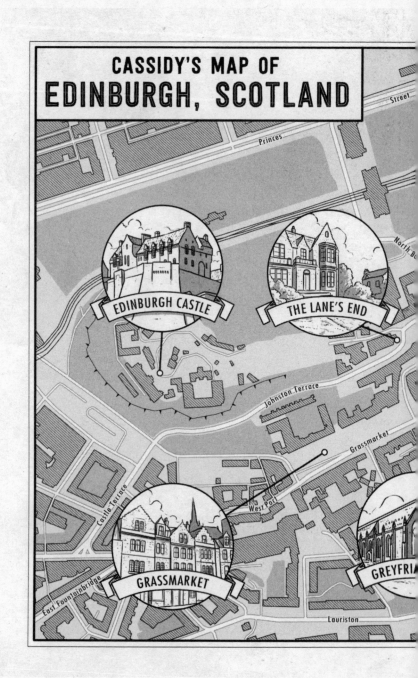

CASSIDY'S MAP OF
EDINBURGH, SCOTLAND

EDINBURGH CASTLE

THE LANE'S END

GRASSMARKET

GREYFRIA

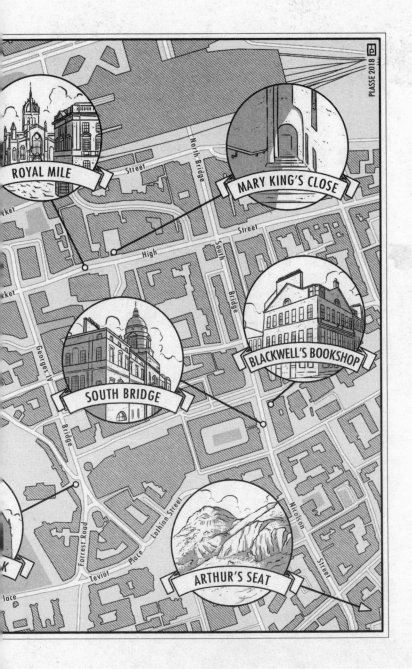

ROYAL MILE

MARY KING'S CLOSE

SOUTH BRIDGE

BLACKWELL'S BOOKSHOP

ARTHUR'S SEAT

PLASSE 2018

PART ONE

THE INSPECTERS

CHAPTER ONE

People think that ghosts only come out at night, or on Halloween, when the world is dark and the walls are thin. But the truth is, ghosts are everywhere. In the bread aisle at your grocery store, in the middle of your grandmother's garden, in the front seat on your bus.

Just because you can't see them doesn't mean they aren't there.

I'm sitting in History class when I feel the *tap-tap-tap* on my shoulder, like drops of rain. Some people call it intuition, others second sight. That tickle at the edge of your senses, telling you there's something *more*.

This isn't the first time I've felt it—not by a long shot. Not even the first time I've felt it here at my school. I've tried to ignore it—I always do—but it's no use. It wears away at my focus, and I know the only way to make it stop is to give in. Go and see for myself.

From across the room, Jacob catches my eye and shakes his head. *He* can't feel that *tap-tap-tap,* but he knows me well enough to know when *I* do.

I shift in my seat, forcing myself to focus on the front of the classroom. Mr. Meyer is valiantly trying to teach, despite the fact it's the last week of school before summer vacation.

". . . Toward the end of the Vietnam War in 1975, US troops . . ." my teacher drones on. Nobody can sit still, let alone pay attention. Derek and Will are sleeping with their eyes open, Matt is working on his latest paper football. Alice and Melanie are making a list.

Alice and Melanie are *popular kids.*

You can tell because they look like copies—same shiny hair, same perfect teeth, same painted nails—where I'm all elbows and knees, round cheeks, and curly brown hair. I don't even own nail polish.

I know you're supposed to *want* to be one of the popular kids, but the truth is, I never have. It just seems like it would be exhausting, trying to keep up with all the rules. Smile, but not too wide. Laugh, but not too loud.

Wear the right clothes, play the right sports, care about things, but never care too much.

(Jacob and I have rules, too, but those are different.)

As if on cue, Jacob stands up and makes his way toward Melanie's desk. *He* could be a popular kid, I think, with his floppy blond hair, bright blue eyes, and good humor.

He shoots me a devilish look before perching on the edge of her desk.

He *could* be, but there's just one problem.

Jacob's dead.

"'Things we need for movie night . . .'" he reads aloud from Melanie's paper. But I'm the only one who can hear him. Melanie folds another sheet, an invitation—I can tell by the capital letters, the pink pen—and reaches forward to pass it to Jenna, who sits in front of her. As Melanie does this, her hand goes straight through Jacob's chest.

He looks down, as if offended, then hops off the desk.

Tap-tap-tap goes the feeling in my head, like a whisper I can't quite hear. Impatient, I check the clock on the wall, waiting for the lunch bell.

Jacob meanders over to Alice's desk next, examining the many multicolored pens she keeps lined up across the top. He leans in close and gingerly brings one of his fingers to the pens, all his focus narrowed on the nearest one as he pokes it.

But the pen doesn't move.

In the movies, poltergeists can lift televisions and slide beds across the floor. But the truth is, it takes a *lot* of spirit power for a ghost to reach across the Veil—the curtain between their world and ours. And the ghosts that do have that kind of strength, they tend to be really old and not very nice. The living may take strength from love and hope, but the dead grow strong on darker things. On pain and anger and regret.

Jacob furrows his brow as he tries—and fails—to flick Matt's paper football.

I'm glad he's not made of all that stuff.

I don't actually know how long Jacob's been *dead* (I think the word quietly, because I know he doesn't like it). It can't have been *that* long, since there's nothing retro about him—he's got on a superhero T-shirt, dark jeans, and high-tops—but he doesn't talk about what happened, and I don't ask. Friends deserve a little privacy—even if he can read my mind. I can't read his, but all things considered, I would rather be alive and not psychic than psychic and a ghost.

He looks up at the word *ghost* and clears his throat. "I prefer the phrase 'corporeally challenged.'"

I roll my eyes because he knows I don't like it when he reads my mind without asking. Yes, it's a weird side effect of our relationship, but come on. Boundaries!

"It's not my fault you think so loud," Jacob replies with a smirk.

I snort, and a few students glance my way. I sink lower in my chair, my sneakers knocking against my book bag on the floor. The invitation Melanie passed to Jenna makes its way around the room. It doesn't stop at my desk. I don't mind.

Summer is almost here, and that means fresh air and sunshine and books to read for fun. It means the annual family trek down to the rented beach house on Long Island so Mom and Dad can work on their next book.

But most of all, it means no hauntings.

I don't know what it is about the beach house—maybe

the fact that it's so new, or the way it sits on a calm stretch of shore—but there seem to be far fewer ghosts down there than here in upstate New York. Which means that as soon as school's out, I get six full weeks of sun and sand and good nights' sleep.

Six weeks without the *tap-tap-tap* of restless spirits.

Six weeks of feeling *almost normal*.

I can't wait for the break.

I can't wait . . . and yet, the moment the bell rings, I'm up, backpack on one shoulder and purple camera strap on the other, letting my feet carry me toward that persistent *tap-tap-tap*.

"Crazy idea," says Jacob, falling into step beside me, "but we *could* just go to lunch."

It's Meat Loaf Thursday, I think, careful not to answer out loud. *I'd rather face the ghosts.*

"Hey, now," he says. But we both know Jacob's not a *normal* ghost, just like I'm not a normal girl. Not anymore. There was an accident. A bike. A frozen river. Long story short, he saved my life.

"Yeah, I'm practically a superhero," Jacob says, right before a locker swings open in his face. I wince, but he passes straight through the door. It's not that I *forget* what Jacob is—it's pretty hard to forget when your best friend is invisible to everyone else. But it's amazing what you can get accustomed to.

And it says something that the fact that Jacob's been haunting me for the past year isn't even the strangest part of my life.

We hit the split in the hall. Left goes to the cafeteria. Right goes to the stairs.

"Last chance for normal," Jacob warns, but he's got that crooked grin when he says it. We both know we passed normal a long time ago.

We go right.

Down the stairs and along another hall, against the flow of lunchtime traffic, and with each turn, the *tap-tap-tap* gets stronger, turning into a pull, like a rope. I don't even have to think about where to go. In fact, it's easier if I *stop* thinking and just let it reel me in.

It draws me to the doors of the auditorium. Jacob

shoves his hands in his pockets and mutters something about bad ideas, and I remind him he didn't have to come, even though I'm glad he did.

"Ninth rule of friendship," he says, "ghost-watching is a two-person sport."

"That it is," I say, snapping the cap off my camera lens. It's a clunky old beast, this camera, a manual with a busted viewfinder and black-and-white film, hanging off my shoulder on its thick purple strap.

If a teacher catches me in the auditorium, I'll say I was taking photos for the school paper. Even though all the clubs have ended for the year . . .

And I never worked for the paper.

I push open the auditorium doors and step inside. The theater is huge, with a high ceiling and heavy red curtains that hide the stage from view.

Suddenly, I realize why the *tap-tap-tap* has led me here. Every school has stories. Ways to explain that creaking sound in the boys' bathroom, that cold spot at the back of the English room, the smell of smoke in the auditorium.

My school's the same. The only difference is that when I hear a ghost story, I get to find out if it's real. Most of the time it's not.

A creaky sound is just a door with bad hinges.

A cold feeling is just a draft.

But as I follow the *tap-tap-tap* down the theater aisle and up onto the stage, I know there's something to this particular story.

It's the one about a boy who died in a play.

Apparently, a long, long time ago, when the school first opened, there was a fire in the second act of *A Midsummer Night's Dream*. The set went up in flames, but everyone got out—or so they thought.

Until they found the boy under the trapdoor.

Jacob shivers beside me, and I roll my eyes. For a ghost, he scares so easily.

"Have you ever thought," he says, "that you don't scare easily enough?"

But I scare just as easily as anyone. Believe it or not, I don't *want* to spend my time searching for ghosts. It's just that if they're *there*, I can't ignore them. It's like knowing there's someone standing right behind you and being told not to turn around. You can feel their breath on your neck, and every second you don't look, your mind just makes it worse because in the end, what you don't see is always scarier than what you do.

I climb onto the stage, Jacob at my heels. I can feel him hesitating, his own reluctance dragging me back as I pull up a corner of the heavy red curtain and slip backstage. Jacob follows, passing straight through the curtain.

It's dark here—so dark it takes a second for my eyes to adjust to the various props and benches scattered across the stage. A thin ribbon of light comes from beneath the curtain. It's quiet, but there's an eerie sense of motion. The faint groan of sandbags settling on their hinges. The whisper of air beneath the floorboards. The rustle of what I hope is paper and not rats.

I know that some of the older kids in school dare each other to go back here. To put their ear to the floor and listen for the boy who didn't make it. I heard them bragging about it once in the hall, how long they'd each lasted. One minute. Two. Five. Some claim they heard the boy's voice. Others say they smelled smoke, heard the footsteps of fleeing children. But it's hard to know where the rumors end and the truth picks up.

Nobody dared *me* to come here. They didn't have to. When your parents write books about paranormal activity, people assume you're weird enough to go on your own.

I guess they're right.

I'm halfway across the darkened stage when I trip over something and stumble forward. Jacob's hand shoots out to catch me, but his fingers go through my arm, and I bang my knee on the wooden floor. My palm smacks hard, and I'm surprised when the floor bounces a little, until I realize I'm on top of the trapdoor.

The *tap-tap-tap* grows more insistent under my hands. Something dances at the edge of my sight: a thin gray curtain caught in a constant breeze. Different from the heavy red stage curtain. This one, no one else can see.

The Veil.

The boundary between this world and somewhere

else, between the living and the dead. This is what I'm looking for.

Jacob shifts his weight from foot to foot. "Let's get this over with."

I get back to my feet.

"Ghost five," I say, for luck. A ghost five is like a high five for friends who can't really touch. It's basically just me putting out my hand and him pretending to hit it, both of us murmuring a soft "smack" sound on contact.

"Oof," says Jacob, pulling his hand away, "you hit too hard."

I laugh. He's such a dork sometimes. But the laughter makes space in my chest, clears out the fear and nerves as I reach for the Veil.

I've seen people on TV—"ghost whisperers"—talk about crossing over, connecting with the other side like it's flipping a switch or opening a door. But for me, it's this—finding the part in the curtain, catching hold of the fabric, and pulling.

Sometimes, when there's nothing to find, the Veil is barely there, more smoke than cloth and hard to catch hold of. But when a place is haunted—*really* haunted—the fabric twists around me, practically pulling me through.

Right here, right now, it dances between my fingers, waiting to be caught.

I grab hold of the curtain, take a deep breath, and pull.

CHAPTER TWO

When I was younger, I used to be afraid of the monster in the closet. I couldn't go to sleep until my dad came in, threw open the closet door, and showed me it was empty. Crossing the Veil is like opening the closet door.

Of course, the difference is, monsters aren't real. The closet was always empty.

The Veil . . . not so much.

A chill washes over my skin. For a second I'm not backstage but underwater, the icy current closing over my head, the light vanishing as something heavy pulls me down, down, down—

"Cassidy."

I blink at the sound of Jacob's voice, and the memory of the river is gone. I'm backstage again, and everything is the same, but different. The stage is faded, like an old photograph, but it's not as dark as it was before. Instead, it's lit up by a handful of spotlights, and I can hear the murmur of an audience beyond the curtain.

Jacob's still at my side, but he looks solid, real. I glance down at myself. As always, I look more or less the same, a little washed-out but still me, down to the camera around my neck. The only real difference is the light inside my chest. A coil of cool, blue-white brightness that shines straight through my ribs, like the filament in a lightbulb.

Like Iron Man, Jacob sometimes jokes. I hold the camera against my front to muffle the glow.

"Places!" calls an adult's voice from the wings, and I jump. Jacob grabs my sleeve to steady me, and this time, his hand doesn't go through. He has more weight, or I have less, but either way I'm grateful for the contact.

"Act two!" the voice adds.

And I know what this is.

When this is.

The night of the fire.

In a flurry, like bats set loose, boys and girls in fairy crowns and glittering capes race across the stage. They don't notice me and Jacob. The curtains come up, and the audience murmurs from the darkened theater. My first urge is to duck, to scramble back into the wings, but I remind myself that the audience isn't really there. This place, this space, this time—it belongs to the ghost. And his memories.

Everything else is just set dressing.

I raise the camera, not bothering to look through the viewfinder (it's cracked). I snap a few quick photos, knowing that the most I'll see on the film is a shadow of what's here. A little more than normal. A little less than truth.

"And to think," whispers Jacob wistfully, "we could be in the cafeteria, having lunch like normal people."

"You can't eat, and I see ghosts," I whisper back as the second act begins. The fairies gather in the makeshift woods around their queen.

I scan the stage, the bridges overhead, the props, searching for the source of the fire. Maybe that's why I'm drawn to places like this. Ghosts stick around for a reason. Maybe, if someone learns the truth—if *I* learn the truth—about what happened, it'll bring them peace. They'll go away.

"That's not how it works," whispers Jacob.

My head snaps toward him. "What do you mean?"

He opens his mouth to answer when a boy appears. He's short, with pale skin and a mop of black curls, and I know he's the one, the ghost—there's just this feeling, like the ground is tipping toward him.

I watch as his cape catches on the ropes and rigging in the wings. He manages to pull free, stumbles onto the stage in front of us, but he drops his crown and has to double back. For a second, his eyes meet mine, and I think he sees me, and I want to say something, but Jacob presses a hand over my mouth and shakes his head.

The music starts, and the boy's eyes cloud, and I watch him take his place.

"We should go," whispers Jacob, but I can't, not yet. I need to know what happened.

As if on cue, I hear the hiss of a rope, and turn to see the rigging—the one the boy got caught on—coming loose, uncoiling. A bag of sand slides, sinks, falls, and as it does, it catches on a power box, knocks a fuse.

There's a spark—just a spark, such a small thing—but as I watch, it leaps to the nearest thing, an unused piece of the paper forest, shoved into the wings.

"Oh no," I whisper as the play continues.

It doesn't start as a fire, not at first. It is only warmth, and smoke. Smoke that goes unnoticed in the darkened theater. I look up and watch the thin tendril spread and thicken and coat the ceiling like a low cloud. Still, no one notices.

Not until, at last, it becomes fire.

There's so much kindling on the stage: a forest made out of wooden planks and gossamer and paint. It catches so fast, and finally the spell of the play is broken. The fairy students scatter and the audience panics, and I know it's just a memory, an echo of something already said and done, but I can *feel* the heat as it spreads.

Jacob grabs my hand, pulling me away from the raging flames.

Even through the panic, my fingers turn the camera crank, snapping photos, eager to catch something as the world around me turns to smoke and fire and panic.

My head is beginning to feel foggy, like I've been holding my breath. I know I've been here long enough, that it's time to go, but my feet won't move.

And then I see the dark-haired boy, trying to stay low, the way you're taught in class, but the fire is spreading so fast, swallowing the set on every side, climbing the curtains. There's nowhere to run, the whole stage is up in flames, so he goes down, shuffles on his hands and knees until he reaches the trapdoor.

"Don't!" I call, but of course, it's useless. He doesn't listen, doesn't turn. He pulls the door up and climbs down into the dark just before a piece of burning set collapses on top of the stage, pinning the trapdoor shut.

"Cassidy," says Jacob, but I can't tear my eyes away from the fire, even as my lungs fill with smoke.

Jacob grabs me by the shoulders.

"We have to *go*," he orders, and when I don't move, he gives me a push and I stumble, falling backward over a wooden bench. By the time I hit the stage floor, it's cold. The fire is gone, as is the light coming from my chest. Jacob crouches over me, ghostly again, and I slump back, breathless.

Sometimes, you see, I get *stuck*.

It's like Neverland in *Peter Pan*—the longer the Lost Boys stayed, the more they forgot. The longer I'm on the wrong side of the Veil, the harder it is to get out.

Jacob crosses his arms. "Are you happy now?"

Happy isn't the right word. The tapping is still there—it never goes away—but at least I know now, what's on the other side. It makes it easier to ignore.

"Sorry." I get to my feet, brushing the invisible ashes from my jeans. I can still taste the smoke.

"Rule number twenty-one of friendship," says Jacob. "Don't leave your friend in the Veil."

The school bell rings as he says it.

Lunch is officially over.

CHAPTER THREE

Before we go any further, I have to back up.

You see, there are three things you need to know.

Thing #1: For as long as I can remember, I've taken pictures.

Dad says that the world is always changing, every second of every day, and so is everything in it, which means that the *you* you are right now is different from the *you* you were when you started reading this sentence. Crazy, right? And our memories change, too. (For instance, I *swear* the teddy bear I had growing up was green, but according to my parents it was orange.) But when you take a photograph, things stay still. The way that they were, is the way that they are, is the way that they will always be.

Which is why I love pictures.

Thing #2: My birthday is in late March, right at that place when the seasons run together. When the sun is warm but the wind is cold, and trees are starting to blossom but the ground hasn't quite thawed. Mom likes to say I was born with one foot in winter and the other in spring. That's why I can't sit still, and why (according to her) I'm always searching for trouble—because I don't belong to one place.

Thing #3: We live in a suburban town surrounded by fields and hills (and a fair number of ghosts) and trees that change color and rivers that freeze for the winter and a hundred picture-perfect landscapes.

These three things don't seem connected, the photos and the time and the place, but they're all important, I promise. Threads in the fabric.

For my eleventh birthday, Mom and Dad gave me my camera, the vintage one you already know about, with a purple strap and an old-school flash and an aperture that you rotate by hand. All the kids at school use their phones as cameras—but I wanted something solid, something real. It was love at first sight, and right away I knew where I wanted to go, what I wanted to shoot.

There's this place a few miles from our house, a cleft in the hills, and when the sun sets, it sets right there, nested between the two slopes like a ball cupped in someone's hands. I'd been there a dozen times, and it never looked the same. I had this idea of going every day for a year, capturing each and every sunset.

And I wanted to start right then.

Remember what I said about being born in March? Well, for the first time that year, it was actually warm enough to ride my bike, even if the air still had a bite to it, as Mom likes to say. So I looped the camera's purple strap around my neck and took off toward the hills on my bike, racing against the sun, tires hissing over half-frozen ground, through the streets and past the soccer fields and onto the bridge.

The bridge. A short stretch of metal and wood suspended over the water, the kind of bridge you had to take turns on because it wasn't wide enough for two cars. I was halfway across when the truck whipped around the curve and hurtled toward me.

I swerved out of the way, and so did the truck, tires screeching as my bike slammed into the railing hard enough to make sparks fly. Hard enough to send me over the handlebars.

And over the railing.

I fell. It sounds simple, doesn't it? Like a stumble, a trip, a skinned knee. But it was twenty feet down into water that had only days before been frozen solid. And when I broke the surface, the force and the cold knocked all the air from my lungs.

My vision went white, and then black, and by the time it came back, I was still sinking, the camera like a lead weight around my neck, pulling me down, down, down. The river darkened, the surface above a shrinking ripple of light. Somewhere, beyond the water, I thought I saw someone, the smudge of a person, all shadow. But then the shadow was gone, and I was still sinking.

I didn't think about dying.

Didn't think about anything except the icy water in my lungs, the pressing weight of the river, and even those things started to fade, and all I thought was, *I'm falling away from the light.* They tell you to go toward it, and I tried, but I couldn't. My limbs were too heavy. There was no air left.

I don't remember what happened next. Not exactly.

The world did a kind of stutter, like when a movie freezes, gets jammed, skips forward, and then I was sitting on the riverbank, gasping for air as a boy crouched beside me, in jeans and a superhero shirt, his blond hair sticking up as if he'd just run his fingers through it.

"That was close," he said.

At the time, I had no idea.

"What happened?" I asked through chattering teeth.

"You fell in," he said. "I pulled you out."

Which didn't make sense, because I was soaked through, but he wasn't even wet. Maybe if I hadn't been shivering so hard, maybe if my eyes weren't aching from the river, maybe if my head wasn't full of ice, I would have noticed his strange gray pallor. The way I could almost, almost, *almost* see through him. But I was too tired, too cold.

"I'm Jacob," he said.

"Cassidy," I said, slumping back onto the bank.

"Hey," he said, leaning over me, ". . . stay awake . . ."

I heard other voices, then the slam of car doors, the skidding of boots down the half-frozen bank, the distant warmth of someone's coat, but I couldn't keep my eyes open. When I woke up, I was in a hospital bed, and Mom and Dad were there, their hands so warm on mine.

Jacob was there, too, sitting cross-legged in a spare hospital chair (it didn't take me long to realize that no one else could see him). My camera was on the bedside table, the purple strap frayed and the viewfinder cracked. It was damaged but not ruined, changed but not destroyed. Kind of like me.

A little special.

A little strange.

Not quite alive but definitely not . . .

I mean, can someone really die if they don't end up dead? Are they really alive if they come back?

The word for that seems like it should be *undead*, but I'm not a zombie. My heart has that steady *thump-thump*, and I eat and sleep and do all the things that go with "living."

Near death. That's what they call it. But I know it wasn't just near.

I was standing right on top of it. Under it. Long enough for my eyes to adjust, the way they would in a dark room. Long enough for me to make out the edges of the space before being dragged back into the bright, cold light.

In the end, I guess Mom was right.

I have one foot in winter and one in spring.

One foot with the living, and one with the dead.

A week later, I found the Veil.

Jacob and I were taking a walk, trying to wrap our heads around our strange connection—I mean, I'd never been haunted before, and he'd never haunted anyone—when it happened.

We were cutting through an empty lot, and all of a sudden I felt it: the *tap-tap-tap* of someone staring, the shivery sensation of a spiderweb on bare skin. I saw the edge of gray cloth at the corner of my sight. I should have looked away, but I didn't. I couldn't. Instead, I felt myself turn *toward* it. I caught the curtain in my hand, and for an instant, I was falling again, crashing through the surface of the river. But I didn't let go.

And when I blinked, Jacob was still next to me, only he looked *solid*, real, and just as confused as I was. And the empty lot wasn't empty anymore. We were standing inside a warehouse, the *crank* and *clank* of metal echoing off the walls, and someone somewhere was sobbing. The Veil itself didn't scare me, but that sound, the sense of walking into someone else's life—or death—scared me, and I pulled free of that place as fast as I could, wiping off the Veil as if it *were* just a spiderweb stuck to my clothes.

I swore I'd never go back.

I thought I was telling the truth.

But a couple of weeks later, I felt it again, the *tap-tap-tap*, the brush of that gray cloth, and before I knew it, I was reaching out, taking hold, pulling the curtain aside, while Jacob groaned and sulked, and grudgingly followed me through.

And here we are, one year later.

For most people, life and death are pretty black-and-white. But something happened that day when Jacob pulled me out of the water. I guess I pulled him out of somewhere, too, and we got tangled up, and now I'm not all alive and he's not all dead.

If we were in a comic book, this would be our origin story.

Some people get a spider bite, or a vat of acid.

We got a river.

CHAPTER FOUR

I mean, obviously *Batgirl*," Jacob is saying, "the reissue, not the original . . ."

"Sure." I scuff my sneakers against the street as we walk home. There are two of us, but only one shadow on the pavement. We're discussing which comics I should pack for Jacob for the beach vacation.

"And we can't forget the new *Skull and Bone* . . ." Jacob adds.

Skull and Bone is Jacob's favorite comic. In it, this dead cowboy named Skull Shooter gets resurrected to hunt down rogue spirits along with his wolfhound (Bone). Jacob continues listing off options, trying to decide between *Thor #31* and *Skull #5*, but I'm not really listening. Something is nagging at me.

Back in the auditorium, when I was thinking that I could help the ghost boy by seeing what happened to him, Jacob said, *That's not how it works.* But Jacob never talks like that, never says *anything* about the Veil. I've always assumed he doesn't *know* why I'm so drawn to it. Or how I can cross over. Or what I'm supposed to do there. But what if he *does* know, and he's just not telling me?

He can hear me now, wondering, doubting.

"Rule number seven," he says. "Don't be nosy."

Yeah, sure, I think. But the very first rule of friendship is *don't keep secrets*.

He sighs. "I can't tell you everything, Cass. There are rules to being a . . ." He makes a sweeping gesture at himself.

"What kind of rules?" I press.

"Rules like rules!" he snaps, face flushing. I hate seeing Jacob upset, so I let it go. Which is to say I totally *don't* stop thinking about it—very loudly, in his direction—but Jacob pretends he can't hear, and I don't ask again out loud.

"You can pick six comics," I say instead.

He pouts, but it's so over-the-top I can tell he's joking. That's what I love about Jacob. Even when he gets mad, it doesn't last. Nothing seems to stick.

"Fine, seven," I say as we reach my street, "but I get final approval. And no *Batman*."

He looks aghast. "You heathen."

I tap my fingers against the camera, wondering if any of the photos I took in the Veil today will come out. I notice there's only one picture left on the roll.

"Smile," I tell him, and Jacob throws up a peace sign. But he doesn't look at the camera when I take the picture. He never does.

"Haven't you heard?" he likes to tease. "Pictures steal souls. Besides, it's not like I'll show up."

Click.

We walk on, and a few minutes later, our house comes into sight, one of those old Victorians that look like they should be haunted.

(It's not haunted.)

(Except for Jacob.)

(And he doesn't count.)

"Rude," he mumbles, following me inside.

I kick off my shoes by the front door, next to a tower of books. More books spill out of the study and into the hall. Some are research—history, religion, myth, and lore—and some are novels. And other books have my parents' names printed on the covers, the titles emblazoned in silver or gold:

THE INSPECTERS.

It's a play on words, you see, because an *inspector* is a person who searches for and examines something, and a *specter* with an *e* is another word for *ghost*. So an *inspecter* is a person who searches for and examines ghosts.

My parents have written a whole series—they're up to volume six now. They're like history books, but with ghost stories mixed in, truth and myth all rolled together. They're pretty popular. I stop and pick up the latest edition, looking at the photo on the back cover: a slim man in a tweed coat, dark hair flecked gray at the temples (that's Dad). He has a notebook under one arm and glasses perched on the edge of his nose. At his side stands a woman in pale slacks and a colorful blouse, her wild dark curls in a messy bun stuck through with pens, and an open book in her hands, the pages ruffling as if caught in a breeze (that would be Mom).

And curled at their feet is a mound of black fur and green eyes. Our cat, Grim.

The overall effect is one part history and one part magic, with a dash of good old-fashioned superstition.

The funny thing is, Dad doesn't even *believe* in ghosts (the books' editor actually likes that Dad's a skeptic, because it keeps the stories "grounded" and more "relatable" to readers). My parents make a good team: Dad's the scholar, and Mom's the dreamer. He focuses on explaining the past, while she spins ghost stories out of *maybe*s and *what-if*s.

And me? I stay out of it.

Because my parents don't know the whole truth about me. I never told them what *really* happened in the river, never told them about the Veil, or the things I see on the other side. It feels like a secret I should keep.

So my parents talk about—or write about—ghosts, but can't actually see them.

I can actually see ghosts, but don't want to talk—or write—about them.

I'm pretty sure that's called *irony*.

"Hello?" I call out. "Anyone here?"

Mom's voice bounces down the hall; she's on the

phone in her study. I can tell by the way she talks that she's doing an interview.

"Do I think there's more to the world than we understand?" Mom rattles on. "Of course. It would be sheer arrogance to think otherwise . . ."

She sticks her head through the doorway (her bun its usual porcupine of pens) and smiles at me but keeps on talking. "Ghosts, residues, spirits, specters, call them what you like . . ." She collars me into a hug without breaking her interview stride. "Sure, science can explain some things, but when different people experience the same supernatural occurrence, see the same ghost, relate the same story, we should ask why."

She turns her face from the phone. "Dad's on his way home," she whispers into my hair. "Don't go far. We need to talk."

We need to talk.

Four words you never want to hear, and I want to ask for a clue, but Mom's already pulling away. "Well, yes," she says to the interviewer, "I have indeed felt the presence of ghosts."

Probably true.

"I've *seen* them."

Jacob waves a hand in front of her face.

Less true.

Weirdly enough, Mom kind of knows about Jacob. There are only so many times you can get away with talking to your invisible best friend before you have to explain who's on the other side of the conversation.

But I don't know if Mom really believes in ghosts, or if she just *wants* to believe because it makes the world more interesting. She says she's had her fair share of paranormal experiences, and that "sensitivity" to the supernatural runs in our family. She says that when it comes to the strange and unexplained, it's important to keep an open mind.

What I *do* know is that she doesn't patronize me about Jacob the way Dad does. She doesn't refer to him as my imaginary friend, and doesn't teasingly ask me how *he's* feeling that day, or what *he* wants for dinner.

If there's something Jacob wants me to say to her, she listens.

My stomach growls from missing lunch, so I duck past

Mom's study into the kitchen and make a PB + B + CC, aka peanut butter, banana, and chocolate chips, aka the best sandwich in world, no matter what Jacob says. (I think he's just jealous he can't eat it.) I shove half in my mouth, put the rest in the fridge for later, and head upstairs.

Our cat, Grim, is asleep on my bed.

Despite the way he looks on my parents' book, in real life, Grim lacks what Mom calls *basic feline dignity*. Right now, for instance, he's sprawled on his back, paws up in the air like a dog playing dead. When I drop my book bag on the floor, he doesn't even twitch. I scratch the cat behind the ears, just to make sure he's still alive, then beeline for the room that used to be my closet.

Dad helped me convert it. We spent a weekend pulling out all the shelves, transforming the small space into a perfect darkroom. There's a table with reels, a developing canister, an enlarger, photo paper, and pans for the chemicals. There's even a steel cable with little clips to hold the drying photos. Everything a photographer needs.

Jacob is already there, because he has no respect for things like doors and stairs.

He shrugs, leaning back against the wall. "Ghost perk—shortcuts."

I lift the camera and crank the film, then thumb open the catch on the back, tipping the canister out into my hand.

And then I close the door, plunging the closet—and us—into total darkness.

Well, it would be total, if Jacob didn't kind of . . . shine. It's not so bright; more like moonlight. It doesn't hurt the film, but it doesn't help me see anything, either, so I still have to trust my hands to do the work.

I pop open the canister and dump the film into my palm. Spool it onto the little metal reel and drop the reel into a developing tank, which is like a short thermos.

Then I flip a switch, and the little closet fills with low red light. It casts both of us in an eerie glow, like something out of a horror movie. (Jacob wiggles his fingers and makes spooky sounds.)

I add water to rinse the film thermos, then developer, swirling the container. While I work, Jacob rambles about whether to pack *Thor #57* instead of *#62*. When the negatives are prepped, I hang them to dry. They won't be ready for a few days.

I pick a negative strip that *is* ready—this one from another recent excursion Jacob and I took, to an abandoned house a few blocks over. The house had been empty for years, but as Jacob and I discovered, it wasn't truly *empty*. I feed the strip into the enlarger (a kind of projector designed to transfer pictures onto photo paper). Then it's on to the printing.

There's a kind of magic to exposing film. It's right there in the word *expose*—to reveal. I feel like a mad scientist as I move the photo paper through trays of developer, stop baths, rinse. And as I poke the paper with the tongs, the first picture finally begins to surface.

My camera may be special, but it's not as strange as I am. I can take it with me into the Veil, but it can't see the way I do. Most of the time, the photos that show up are ordinary: a black-and-white translation of my full-color world.

But now and then, I get lucky.

Now and then, the camera catches a shadow against a wall, the lines like smoke around a body, a door to some-place that's no longer there.

Jacob hovers at my shoulder.

"You're breathing on me," I whisper.

"Am not," he says.

"Are too."

His breath is cold, a chill in the stuffy room, but my attention drifts back to the trays.

One by one, the photos come into focus.

There's a shot of the abandoned house from the outside, sunlight cutting through warped wood.

And one from inside, a straight shot down a dark-ened hall.

And then—

A winner.

It's a photo taken from the other side of the Veil—I can tell by the faint gray sheen. And there, at the top of the stairs, the smudge of a ghostly girl in a nightgown.

Jacob whistles softly.

If I showed this picture to anyone, they'd just assume it was photoshopped. And even if they believed me, the truth is, I wouldn't want this on display. I don't want to be like those TV mediums who stand onstage and pretend to communicate with the dead. And it's not as if the dead really *speak* to me (Jacob aside).

"I could be your interpreter," he offers.

I snort. "No thanks."

I glance back at my fresh negatives from today, and wonder if I caught a glimpse of the boy in his cape and crown, ghosted on the curtain.

I'm stiff from hunching over the equipment, and I kill the red light and step out into the bedroom, blinking at the sudden brightness.

Jacob throws himself down on the bed next to Grim. There's no bounce, no dent in the comforter, but Grim's ear twitches, and a few moments later, he paws at the air around Jacob. We've never been able to figure out if Grim actually *sees* him or just kind of senses a disturbance in the force.

Cats are weird like that.

I decide to start packing for the beach, and drag my suitcase out from under my bed. I sort through my summer clothes while Jacob pretends to rub a smudge of dirt from the hem of his T-shirt. I can't imagine having to wear the same clothes for the rest of my li—um, existence.

Jacob shrugs. "I'm just glad I was in a Captain America mood that day."

That day. What happened that day? I wonder if he'll ever tell me.

Jacob doesn't acknowledge the thought. He just rolls onto his stomach and starts reading whatever comic I left open on the bed.

He spends a few seconds trying to *will* the page to turn before I reach over and do it for him.

"One of these days," he mumbles.

Downstairs, I hear the front door open and close. A few seconds later, Dad calls up.

"Family meeting!"

CHAPTER FIVE

F *amily meeting.*

Words, much like *we have to talk*, that *never* bring good news.

There's a fresh pasta-pizza on the table, which is another bad sign. Pasta-pizza—also known as marinara sauce, meatballs, and cheese on a garlic bread crust—is my favorite food, and Mom and Dad only order it from Dino's on special occasions, or when something really bad has happened. It's confusing, the way parents do that—there should be good news food and bad news food, so you know what you're in for.

Mom's pulling down plates and Dad's setting the table when I walk in, both of them making a lot of noise without saying much.

". . . oh, I took that interview with Channel Five . . ."

"How did it go?"

"Fine, fine . . . Did you print out that contract?"

Jacob hops up on the counter, legs swinging silently against the cupboards as I load a slab of pizza onto my plate. He considers the concoction of cheese and sauce and meatball goodness.

"That's disgusting."

You mean amazing, I think, lifting it to my mouth.

I take a massive bite. Cheese burns the roof of my mouth, and Mom snaps her fingers, a wordless reprimand for eating before everyone is at the table. Dad catches me around the shoulders in a one-arm hug. He smells like clean shirts and old books.

When we're all sitting, I notice another red flag: Mom and Dad aren't eating. They're not even *pretending* to eat. I force myself to put the pasta-pizza down.

"So," I say, aiming for casual, "what's up?"

Mom draws a purple pen from her bun, puts it back. "Oh, not much . . ." she says. Dad shoots her a look, as if she's abandoned him.

"Cassidy . . ." he starts, breaking out my full name. "We have some news."

Oh god, I think, *I'm going to be a big sister.*

Jacob crinkles his nose in disgust, and I'm so

44

convinced this is the news that I'm totally caught off guard when Dad says, "We're going to have a TV show."

I stare dumbly. "What?"

"Do you remember when the first *Inspecters* book came out," says Mom, "and there was quite a bit of press? And some people thought it would make a good show? There was a production company that bought the rights . . ."

"Yeah," I say slowly. "But I also remember you telling me that it would never actually happen."

Mom fidgets.

Dad rubs his neck.

"Well," he says simply. "There have been some developments in the last few weeks. We didn't want to tell you in case it all fell through, but . . ." He looks to Mom as if for help.

She takes over, flashing a high-wattage smile. "It's really happening!"

My mind goes blank. I don't know what this means. For them. For us. For me.

"Okay," I say, unsure what the catch is. I mean, it's big

news, but I don't see why they were so nervous to tell me. "That's great! Who's going to play you?"

Dad chuckles. "No one," he says. "That is, we're going to play ourselves."

I frown. "I don't understand."

"It's not a *show* show," Dad explains. "It's more like a documentary."

Mom can't hide her enthusiasm now. "It'll be just like the books, your dad with the facts and me with the legends," she says, talking a mile a minute. "Every episode will focus on a different city, a different set of sites and stories . . ."

My head spins, and I'm trying to figure out if I'm excited or horrified or a bit of both. All I can think of are those ghost TV shows. You know, where people stand in pitch-black rooms lit only by night-vision cameras, and whisper into mics? Is that what my parents' show will be like?

"And *you* won't have to be on camera," Mom is saying to me, "not unless you really want to be, but you'll be with us every step of the way, and we can go to the beach another time—"

"Wait, what?" I shake my head, my summer plans falling apart. "When does this start?"

Dad frowns. "Well, the thing is, the schedule's kind of been fast-tracked. They want us at the first location next week."

Next week. When we're supposed to be at the beach.

"Um. That's really soon," I say, trying to keep the panic from my voice. "Where are we going?"

"All over," says Mom, producing a folder with *The Inspecters* printed across the front. " 'The Most Haunted Cities in the World,' that's the show's theme."

The world, I think, *is a very big place.*

"I'm more concerned about the *most haunted cities* part," says Jacob.

For a ghost, he really isn't a fan of scary things, or haunted places, or *anything* to do with the Veil.

For a long time, I didn't understand why. I *wondered* a lot, but I didn't want to ask. And then, one day, he must have gotten tired of my thinking it, because he came out and told me.

"It's . . . cold," he said. "Like, if you walk out into the snow, but you're warm, you don't start shivering right

47

away. You've got all that heat to lose. But I feel like I just came in, and going back out there, into the cold, I feel like I'll never get warm again."

I wish I could slip my hand into his.

Give him some of my warmth.

But all I can do is promise that I won't let him freeze.

That I'll never leave him behind.

Where you go, I go, I think.

"Well, Cass?" asks Dad, the light catching on his glasses so it looks like he's winking at me.

So much for a ghost-free summer.

"What do you think?" presses Mom.

Which isn't a fair question. Not at all. Parents love to ask that when you don't really have a choice. I think it sounds crazy, and scary. I think I'd rather go to the beach.

But Mom and Dad look so excited, and I don't want to ruin that. Plus—I shoot a look at Jacob—it *could* be fun.

He groans.

Mom opens the folder, and my eyes track across the first page.

THE INSPECTERS
EPISODE ONE
LOCATION: Edinburgh, Scotland

What do I know about Scotland? It's north of England, which is an ocean away. It has people in kilts, and . . . that's about it.

I keep reading, and come to the episode's title:

CITY OF GHOSTS

"Well, that's not ominous," snipes Jacob as a thrill runs through me, half nerves and half anticipation.

I thought my life was already pretty weird.

Apparently, it's about to get weirder.

PART TWO

CITY OF GHOSTS

CHAPTER SIX

C assidy! The cab's here!"

   I shove the last of my things into my suitcase and sit on the lid to make it close. I was supposed to be packing for the beach. Bathing suits and shorts and sunscreen and a summer without hauntings. Instead, I've shoveled sweaters and boots into my bag. According to the weather app on my phone, Scotland's definition of summer is cold and rainy with a chance of hail.

Jacob perches on the edge of the bed in his usual T-shirt and jeans, because ghosts don't need raincoats.

"You have the comics, right?" he asks.

"They're in my backpack."

"Do you have room for one more, because I was thinking, we don't have any *Justice*—"

"No," I say, double-checking my camera bag for film. "I'm cutting you off."

Dad appears in the doorway, a suitcase in one hand and the cat carrier in the other. Grim glowers from the depths of his cage.

"Who are you talking to?" Dad asks.

"Just Jacob," I say.

Dad looks around in an exaggerated way so I can tell he's just humoring me. "And is *Jacob* ready to go?"

"Negative," answers Jacob from the bed. "This is a terrible idea."

"Oh yeah," I say emphatically. "He's dying to see all the haunted houses, and haunted caves, and haunted castles."

Jacob glares. "Traitor."

"I'm glad," says Dad brightly. "I can't promise any ghosts, but there certainly is a wealth of history."

Grim hisses in protest.

I zip up my suitcase and haul it down the stairs with a stubborn *thud thud thud*, through the open door, and down the steps to the waiting cab. I look back at our house, feeling a pang of nerves as Dad locks the front door.

"It'll still be here when we get back," says Mom, reading my face. "This is just a change of setting, a new storyline, a fresh chapter. We have a whole book to write," she says, squeezing me around the shoulders, "and how do we write it?"

"One page at a time," I say automatically.

It's Mom's favorite saying, and ever since my dip in the river, I've tried to hold on to it like a rope. Every time I get nervous or scared, I remind myself that every good story needs twists and turns. Every heroine needs an adventure.

So we pile into the cab, two parents, one girl, a ghost, and a ticked-off cat, and we head for the airport.

Mom and Dad spend most of the drive talking about the upcoming schedule. The show has hired a local film crew and guide, and given us one week to shoot whatever we need. Dad is holding a folder with the history of the locations, and Mom has a notebook full of scribbles that no one else can read. The more I listen to them talking about the logistics, the more I realize this show has been in the works for *months*, even if it just came together.

Nothing happens until it happens, and then it's already happening. That's one of Dad's sayings.

The cab pulls up to the airport. But when we climb out, we're no longer two parents, one girl, a ghost, and a ticked-off cat.

Because Jacob's gone.

He does this sometimes. Vanishes. I don't know if he's sulking or just taking a shortcut. The first time he disappeared, we were driving down the East Coast in search of haunted lighthouses for my parents' most recent book. One minute he was there, and the next, he was gone. I freaked out, afraid he was somehow bound to the river, that he'd hit some invisible boundary ten or twenty miles out of town and gotten stuck.

But when we arrived at the first lighthouse, there he was, sitting on the steps.

"What?" he said defensively. "I get carsick."

Such a Jacob answer.

I wonder where he really goes, what he does without me; I wonder if ghosts need sleep, if he has to return to the Veil to recharge, or if he's just being ornery.

But as my parents and I check our luggage, go through security, and board the airplane, there's still no sign of him. And as I sit in my window seat and watch the ground fall away during takeoff, I really wish he'd stayed.

"Ladies and gentlemen, the seat belt sign is now on . . ."

The sun's just coming up as I open my eyes and press my face to the window. It's hard to imagine that there is a literal ocean beneath us. A new world waiting on the other side. A world full of secrets, and mysteries, and ghosts.

The strangest thing is that way up here, thirty-five thousand feet in the air, wrapped inside this metal bird, I can't feel the Veil. There's no *other side* tickling my senses, no gray cloth at the edge of my sight, and it leaves me feeling like I'm missing a piece of myself. Peter Pan severed from his shadow.

It doesn't help that Jacob's not here.

I try not to worry. He always shows back up eventually.

The plane gives a small rattle, a turbulent shake, and Grim glares at me from the crate under the seat in front of me. He doesn't make a sound, but his green eyes narrow as if I'm personally responsible for his current imprisonment.

Dad's out cold, but Mom's awake and skimming a book called *Spirits, Specters, Scotland*. It looks pretty cheesy—the cover shows a castle under a full moon, and tendrils of fog that turn to badly photoshopped spirits. But I find myself reading over her shoulder, and I notice there's a section on Edinburgh.

The city—which, it turns out, is pronounced *Eh-din-bur-uh* and not *Eh-din-berg*—is more than *nine hundred* years old. There's an illustrated map, complete with parks and bridges, churches, and even a *castle*. Still, the city is smaller than I expected, only a few miles across, and split into an *Old Town* and a *New Town*.

"New Town is relative," Mom explains when she catches me reading. "It's still more than two hundred years old. Old Town," she adds giddily, "is where all the best ghosts are."

"And where are we staying?" I ask. I know the answer

before her finger lands on the map, right in the middle of Old Town.

Great, I imagine Jacob saying as I lean back in my seat.

I stare out the window as daylight creeps into the sky. I think about Jacob again, and start to worry about ghosts not being able to cross running water. As the plane descends, the worry weighs on my chest. By the time we land, I'm starting to panic.

There's no Jacob on the jet bridge.

No Jacob in the terminal.

No Jacob on the escalator or at the baggage claim.

And then the luggage starts tumbling out onto the carousel, and the first thing I see isn't the red and yellow stripes of my suitcase (yes, I'm a Gryffindor), but the boy riding cross-legged on top of it. He loves making an entrance.

I sag with relief. Jacob hops down, shoves his hands in his pockets, and flashes me a crooked smile.

"Ghost perk," he says, and I can't decide if I want to throw my arms around him or slug him in the shoulder. Lucky for him, I can't do either.

We pile into a black cab, and Grim pancakes himself on the bottom of his carrier and glowers at Jacob, who makes faces back as Mom gives the driver the address of the place we're staying.

We drive for a few minutes through ordinary-looking streets lined with grocery stores and hair salons and banks. And then, out of nowhere, the road changes beneath us, shifting from pavement to cobblestones, as if we're moving back in time. The car rattles over the uneven road. Grim looks venomous, and Jacob looks queasy.

The cab driver says something, but his accent is so thick that it takes me a moment to realize he's talking to us instead of singing a song to himself. Dad starts nodding absently, pretending to understand. But I manage to pick apart the driver's melodic voice into words. A question.

"What brings you to bonnie Scotland?"

Mom must have caught it, too, because she sits forward and says, "Ghosts."

Back home, that one word would be enough to kill the conversation, but the cabbie doesn't even seem fazed.

"Ah," he says casually. "Saw a ghost up north once."

Mom brightens. "Really?"

"Och, aye," he says with a nod. "The wife and I went to the Highlands for a day, and having taken the air and seen all there was to see, we made our way to a nearby castle in search of some refreshment."

Nothing strange about that, I think.

"Now, the kitchens in this castle had been turned into a tavern, all stone and glass and blazing hearth, and three low chairs were set round the fire," the cab driver goes on. "Two of the chairs were empty, and there was a man sitting in the third, watching the fire. A gentlemanly sort. My wife had her eye on a table in the back, and I had the drinks in my hands, so I was following behind, and the space was narrow and I'm not so small, and I knocked into the chair with the man sitting in it. Nearly spilled my beer on him. I said sorry, and my wife, she turned back and asked me who I was talking to.

"And wouldn't you know . . ." He hesitates, the air in the cab as tight as a breath held in too long. "There was no one there. All three chairs were empty."

Dad looks deep in thought, as if it's a riddle, but

Mom's eyes shine like a little kid's at a campfire. Jacob and I shoot each other a wary look. It's one thing for a ghost to nudge an object or fog a bathroom mirror. But to *show up* in our world like that, as if they're flesh and blood? Only Jacob does that, and only for me, and only because we're tangled. So chances are, the cabbie's pulling our leg, or his eyes were playing tricks on him. There's a reason people think they see ghosts in the dark, when lights and shadows can mess with your sight.

The cabbie's gaze meets mine in the rearview mirror. "Don't believe me, lass?" he asks with a smile. "That's all right. Stay in Scotland long enough, and you'll have stories of your own."

Little does he know, I have plenty.

The cab rounds a corner, and we're suddenly face-to-face with the castle from Mom's map. Only it's not a tiny illustration. It's a *real-life castle*. On a *cliff*. I stare, wide-eyed. Dad lets out a small, appreciative whistle. Mom beams. Even Jacob looks impressed. It seems painted on the sky, postcard-perfect.

"Stunning, innit?" says the cabbie.

I remember from the map that the castle is in Old Town, and sure enough we drive over a bridge (there's no water beneath, just a train station and a large green park) and into the older part of the city.

The cabbie turns off the bustling streets and down a slope.

"Here we are," he says, stopping in front of an old stone building with a bright red door. "The Lane's End."

CHAPTER SEVEN

The Lane's End reminds me of that scene in *Harry Potter and the Order of the Phoenix*, where Harry arrives at the Order's headquarters—which is actually Sirius Black's house—but it's hidden by a spell. One of the wizards taps on the stones out front, and the buildings slide apart to reveal the headquarters sandwiched between.

The Lane's End is like that, a gray building tucked between two other gray buildings. Together they sit like books on a shelf, their stone spines running along without any gaps between, their rooftops dotted by chimneys.

When we ring the bell on the bright red door, an older woman answers. She has rosy cheeks and fair skin, and a fat white cat twining between her ankles.

"Oh, hello," says the woman. "You must be the

Blakes. I'm Mrs. Weathershire. I run the Lane's End. Come in."

The foyer walls are covered in old-fashioned portraits, faces that stare off into space. An arched doorway on the right leads into a sitting room, and at the end of the hall, a steep wooden staircase rises up like a tree. As Mrs. Weathershire rattles off details about our stay, I wander toward the stairs.

Jacob falls into step beside me. "I bet it's haunted."

He thinks everything is haunted. With the Lane's End, it's hard to tell. It's *old*, sure, but old doesn't always mean—

A pipe rattles in the walls, and footsteps sound overhead.

Jacob raises his eyebrows.

Well, maybe.

At the base of the stairs, I let my eyes trail up to the landing, only to find a girl staring down at me.

She's about my age, dressed in a crisp white button-down and a pleated skirt. She has light-brown skin, and glossy black hair pulled back into a neat braid. She stares at me, unblinking, and I stare back, because there's something strange about her. Familiar. I can't shake the feeling I've seen her before, even though I *know* I haven't.

"Cassidy!" calls Dad.

I tear my gaze away and backtrack, passing Grim's crate. Mrs. Weathershire's fluffy white cat is sticking a curious paw through the bars. Grim shoots me a look that is half pleading, half murder, and I scoop up the crate and take it with me into the sitting room.

The ceiling is high, the walls lined with books, and there's a fireplace flanked by a pair of couches and capped by a chair. The layout reminds me of the three seats in the cab driver's story, but there's no gentleman ghost, just Mom and Dad and Mrs. Weathershire.

I set down Grim's cage and sink onto one of the sofas, then yelp when I keep sinking, the cushion folding around me like quicksand.

Mom offers her hand and hauls me out as Mrs. Weathershire sets a teapot and a tray on the table. My stomach rumbles—no matter how much food you eat on a plane, you never feel satisfied.

"Biscuits?" Mrs. Weathershire offers, passing me a plate of what are definitely *cookies*. She can call them whatever she wants, so long as I can help myself.

I'm just reaching for the plate when the footsteps sound again overhead.

This time, we all look up.

"Oh, don't mind that," says Mrs. Weathershire. "It's probably just my husband."

"Will we be meeting him?" asks Dad.

Our host gives a small laugh. "I shouldn't think so. Mr. Weathershire's been dead for nigh on eight years." Her smile never even wavers. "Tea?"

Jacob gives me a long look, and I don't need to be able to read his mind to know what he's thinking.

Definitely haunted.

He may be right, but I'm not about to find out. I have a rule about crossing the Veil in places where I have to sleep—I don't do it. Sometimes it really is better *not* to know.

"Now," says Mrs. Weathershire, pouring tea, "what brings you to our fair city?"

"As a matter of fact," says Mom, "we're filming a show about ghosts."

"Oh," says our host, taking up her cup. "Well, you won't have to look far. My Reginald was quite fond of Edinburgh's dead. Bit of an obsession, really." She nods at the bookshelves that line the sitting room wall. "Went around collecting stories from locals for years, kept them in those logs there."

Mom perks up at the mention of stories, while Dad brightens at the mention of something with a written record. "Really?" Dad says, already halfway to his feet. "May I?"

"Help yourself."

When Dad's collected a stack of journals and Mom's finished her tea and I've eaten enough cookies to feel vaguely sick, Mrs. Weathershire rises from her seat.

"Well, then," she says, "I'll show you to your flat . . ."

A *flat* is apparently the British word for an apartment, even though there's nothing flat about the three flights of stairs we have to climb to get there. When we reach the first landing, there's no sign of the black-haired girl, or anyone else.

Mom informs me that in Scotland, an elevator is called a *lift*, which would actually make sense, if the building had one. Mom also explains that the Lane's End is a *lodging house*, which is apparently like a small hotel full of apartments—I mean *flats*—instead of regular hotel rooms. There are two flats per floor, and when we reach the third landing, Mrs. Weathershire finally stops before a door with a brass *3B* and produces an old-fashioned key.

"Here we are . . ."

The door groans open with a noise like a scary movie sound effect, but the space beyond is cozy and clean. There are two bedrooms, and a living room with an old hearth fire, a sofa that looks less likely to eat me, and a writing desk beneath a large window.

Mom and Dad linger on the landing, chatting with Mrs. Weathershire.

"If you need anything," she's saying, "I'm just down on the first floor . . ."

Meanwhile, I free Grim from his travel crate. He darts under the sofa, and I wander over to the window above the desk. The glass is fogged up, but when I run my hand across the cool surface, I'm startled to find the castle waiting on the other side. It looms over a landscape of peaked rooftops and stone chimneys, and I'm struck all over again by the view: more fairy tale than ghost story.

"Jacob," I say softly, "you've really got to see this."

But Jacob doesn't answer.

I turn around. He's not there. I check the bathroom, and find a claw-foot tub. (It literally has monstrous talons for feet, like the bottom half of a gargoyle that's been hollowed out.) But no Jacob.

"Jacob?" I hiss, checking the first bedroom. Nothing.

I enter the second one and find him standing at the foot of the bed, his eyes trained on something hidden behind the door.

"Jacob?"

He doesn't blink, doesn't move.

As I slip behind him into the room, I see what he's staring at: a mirror.

A large mirror in a gilt frame propped against the wall.

At first I think he has seen something strange in the reflection, but then I realize it's the reflection *itself* that's snagged his attention. I follow his gaze and go still, the hair on my arms standing on end.

There are two Jacobs, the one beside me and the one in the mirror, but they're not the same. The Jacob beside me is the one I know. But the one in the mirror is grayed out and gaunt, his shirt and jeans soaked, river water pooling at his feet. I'm not easily spooked these days, but seeing him like that, it scares me. The Jacob in the mirror looks dea—I stop. I don't let myself think the word.

"Jacob," I say, but my voice doesn't seem to register. His eyes are focused and empty at the same time, and I reach out to shake his shoulders, but of course my hands go straight through. In the end I have to step between him and his reflection, breaking his line of sight. *"Jacob."*

He blinks, taking a small, shuffling step back.

"What *was* that?" I ask.

His words are slow, sluggish. "I . . . don't know . . ."

He shivers, as if cold, and turns away, drifting out of the room without another word. I turn back to the mirror, half expecting to see the other Jacob still standing there.

But it's just me.

I head into the living room, where Dad is charging his phone and Mom is unpacking. Jacob is perched on the sofa, his gaze still strange and distant.

Are you okay? I think, collapsing onto the couch beside him.

He nods absently.

Outside, the sun vanishes behind clouds, and the room suddenly darkens. It's like stepping through the Veil—everything goes gray, ominous.

Mom puts her hands on her hips and looks around. "This is delightful," she says, without even a hint of sarcasm. She turns to me. "Any sign of our resident ghost?"

I assume she means Mr. Weathershire and not Jacob, so I shake my head.

"Probably just a large cat and some old pipes," says Dad.

Mom winds her hair into a messy bun. "You're no fun," she says, kissing his cheek.

"You're twice as much," he retorts, cleaning his glasses.

I stifle a yawn. A second later, Dad yawns, too.

"Don't you dare!" chirps Mom. "We have to stay awake. It's the only way to fight jet lag."

Jet lag is apparently what happens when you fly overseas at night, and your body hasn't had time to catch up with the clocks.

I curl up against the couch while Dad calls the producers to let them know we've arrived. The crew is flying in tomorrow from London, and they'll come to meet us, as will our local guide. Dad wanders into the bedroom, talking logistics (but I suspect he really just wants to take a nap). I yawn again and close my eyes, but Mom grabs my shoulder.

"Come on," she says, dragging me to my feet. "It's such a nice day."

I glance out the window. "It looks like rain."

But Mom's not having it. She tosses a raincoat into my arms. "Good thing we came prepared."

I glance back at the couch, but Jacob is gone, and before I can go looking for him, Mom hooks her arm through mine, hauling me toward the door. I only manage to get free long enough to grab my camera.

As we step out into the gray day, a fine mist fills the street, turning people to shadows. Gulls screech by. Somewhere in the distance, a church bell rings.

So this is Scotland, I think.

How haunted can it be?

CHAPTER EIGHT

Torture! Murder! Mayhem!"

A man in a top hat and tattered suit spreads his arms wide.

"Learn the city's darkest secrets in the Edinburgh Dungeon!"

Bagpipes echo on the air and a woman in a dark dress leans against a pole with a lantern on top.

"Ghost tours, every night," she says, "starting at dusk. Look for the lantern."

"Come to Mary King's Close!" announces another man in an old-fashioned cloak.

"Learn the tale of Burke and Hare!"

"Follow in the steps of the city's dead!"

Mom and I are walking down the Royal Mile. It's a broad and busy road that runs from the castle all the way down to the base of a giant hill called Arthur's Seat.

They stand like bookends, the castle and the hill, on either end of the city.

Mom is giddy, caught up in all the hustle and noise. But I feel like I'm losing my mind, because underneath the bustle, I can hear the nagging *tap-tap-tap* of ghosts, some faint and others close, and all of it coming from every side, a low, steady beat like the city has a pulse.

I keep my hand on Mom's arm as we weave through the crowd. Most parents have to keep an eye on their children, to keep them from wandering off, but I've always had to keep an eye on her. Dad's the sort to memorize directions, but Mom prefers to get lost.

How else will you find anything new? she always says.

Mom ducks into a tourist shop to grab us bottles of water, and I hang back on the curb, snapping photos of the street performers and the crowds. I photograph the woman in white who stands on top of a pillar and wails an eerie song, her voice rising and falling. The old man clutching a bouquet of black paper roses with words written on the petals. A man wearing a kilt and playing the bagpipes: a haunting, wind-like tune.

It's all for show, of course, meant to fill the streets

x

with an eerie air. But beyond the act, I can *feel* the ghostly pull of the Veil. It's usually a thing I have to reach for, but here, now, amid the chaos of the Royal Mile, it reaches for me. Puts a hand on my shoulder, pulls me close. Gray threads dance in my sight, but I don't lean in. Instead, I pull my raincoat tight around me and scan the street, taking in shops and pubs, churches and liquor stores, and—

My eyes snag on a row of cameras in a window, and my heart quickens. It's a photo store. BELLAMY'S, reads the curling script across the large glass window. I take a mental picture of where we are so I can find my way back when I've finished the roll of film.

Mom reappears with bottles of water, a candy bar, and a sightseeing booklet.

"Come on, Cass. I've found something you'll love."

I brace myself for something creepy or ghoulish, but Mom leads me down the road to a place called the Elephant House, a bright red café with a banner that proudly announces:

Birthplace of Harry Potter

"No way," I say, following her inside.

I'm in awe as Mom and I explore the café.

Apparently, it was here at the Elephant House where author J. K. Rowling—*the* J. K. Rowling—dreamed up Harry, and Hermione, and Ron.

Here, she sat at one of the wooden tables and created Hogwarts, and Azkaban, and Diagon Alley.

Here, she invented Quidditch, and the Triwizard Tournament, and the Deathly Hallows.

Even the tiny bathrooms tell a story. They are *covered* in thank-you notes. So many languages and handwritings that they all blur into a tapestry of love: a permanent monument to a legendary series of books.

By the time we step back out onto the street, I am beaming. Edinburgh is officially my favorite place.

Then the clouds overhead begin to darken. An ominous wind sweeps through my hair.

"I think it's about to rain," I say, shivering.

Mom shrugs. "This is Scotland. It's always about to rain." She studies her booklet again.

It must be the lingering magic of the Elephant House, because when she says we should visit something called Greyfriars Kirk, I agree.

Only when we're walking do I realize I have no idea what a *kirk* is.

"It's a church," says Mom, adding cheerfully, "and this one's home to the most haunted graveyard in Europe!"

And just like that, the whimsy of the wizarding world is gone, replaced by the threat of specters and spirits. As Mom and I make our way to the graveyard, I can practically hear Jacob in my head, uttering a low, sarcastic *yaaaaay*.

The iron gate sits between two stone columns, metal letters curling overhead.

GREYFRIARS

Beyond the gate, I see stretches of green lawn, the stained-glass windows of a church, people wandering the grounds. I breathe in and taste damp stone, old dirt.

But as we near the gate itself, I grind to a halt.

It's not what I see or taste that worries me. It's what I *feel*.

The air goes thick, and the pressure builds inside my head, the weight of the Veil no longer an arm around my shoulders but a wet blanket, heavy, smothering. Gray cloth billows in front of my eyes.

Mom gives a cheerful squeak and shows me her forearm, where all the hairs are standing on end.

"Look!" she says brightly. "Goose bumps."

I have goose bumps, too, but for a different reason.

As haunted as the Royal Mile was, it didn't feel like *this*.

The Veil isn't inherently scary, or bad. It's just another kind of space. But the energy here is dark and menacing. I'm about to tell Mom we should head back, but she's already got her arm looped through mine, ushering me across the threshold and inside the graveyard walls. Even though I haven't crossed the Veil, it still feels like we've stepped out of one world and into another.

There's a tour group just inside the gate. The guide gestures to one of the graves, where dog toys are piled on the dirt.

"One of Greyfriars's most famous tenants," explains the guide in a posh British accent, "was a terrier named Bobby. But unlike most of the residents, he was very much alive when he first came to the graveyard . . ."

Mom and I hover at the back of the group, listening.

"It's said that when his owner died and was buried here, Bobby stayed by the grave, not for one night, or two, but for fourteen *years*. When he finally passed away—"

A collection of sad *"awws"* from the group.

"—he was buried just within the gate." The guide's expression sobers. "Bobby is probably the kindest ghost you'll find among these stones. Greyfriars is home to the bones of the murdered and the murderers alike." He stops talking, lets the silence grow tense, then claps his hands. "Now, you've got one hour to have a look around. Try to avoid the poltergeist up on the hill."

The tourists break into smaller groups and wander up and down the paths.

Mom brightens at the promise of a poltergeist. "Now *that* we've got to see."

"You go ahead," I tell her. "I'll stick to the normal graves."

"Okay," she says. "Just don't go too far."

She bounces off, with all the enthusiasm of someone rushing toward cake, not corpses.

I turn, surveying the rise and fall of the graveyard. Tombstones are everywhere. They line the grave-yard walls, as tall as coffins turned upright, and stick out of the ground like teeth. Some gravestones are new (well, relatively new) and others are little more than jag-ged bits of broken rock, slabs of concrete half-swallowed by green grass.

A skull and crossbones sits beside a carved angel. A stone reaper looms over a set of anchors. A hangman's noose, a cherub, a bouquet of stone roses. Here and there small gifts have been set on top of gravestones or left in the tangled weeds—bells and trinkets and folded bits of paper.

Don't go too far, Mom said, and I don't mean to, but with every step, the Veil gets heavier, folding around me like river-wet clothes, like icy air . . .

My lungs ache, and my vision goes gray, and by the time I realize what's about to happen, it's already happening.

I'm being pulled through.

CHAPTER NINE

I hear the scrape of handlebars, feel the rush of cold water in my lungs—and then I'm on the other side. The tourists are gone and the graveyard stretches, grim and empty.

This has never happened before.

Sure, I've been places where the Veil felt strong, but never strong enough to reach out and grab me, never strong enough to pull me through.

I look down and see the coil of bluish light glowing through my chest. A tendril of fog circles my knees. It feels wrong, being here without Jacob, and I turn, already looking for the way back, but my feet feel rooted to the damp ground.

The grass rustles, and my pulse spikes, but it's just a terrier, trotting between tombstones—Greyfriars Bobby, the dog who lay down on his owner's grave.

I catch more movement, up at the top of the slope. There, a man paces outside of a crypt, smoking a pipe and muttering to no one. Shadows wick around his edges, smudging the air black.

The poltergeist, I think, remembering Mom's excitement. But he doesn't stray from his crypt, and I'm starting to think this place isn't so bad, when someone screams.

I spin, and the Veil ripples around me as more figures take shape in the fog. A man being hauled toward a platform, where a noose hangs waiting. I turn away, only to find a procession of people making its way through the front gates.

I shouldn't be here, I need to go, need to pull myself out of the Veil, and I'm about to—when I see the woman watching me.

The first thing I notice is the color of her cloak—a red so bright it's like a tear in the gray fabric of the Veil. She moves through the graveyard, wisps of black hair curling like fingers around her hood. Her skin, where it shows, is milk white, her lips crimson.

I want to take a photo, but my hands hang useless at my sides.

Somewhere beyond the Veil, church bells begin to ring.

Somewhere beyond the Veil, someone calls my name, but the voice is far away and fading, and I can't take my eyes from the woman in red.

She is staring straight at me. Not past me, the way other ghosts do, but *at* me, and it's like a finger down my spine. Her dark eyes travel over my front, landing on the curl of light inside my chest.

The look that crosses her face is *hungry*.

"*Cassidy . . .*" comes the voice again, but it falls away as the woman in red begins to hum.

Her voice cuts through the graveyard, low and smooth and sweet. It's like someone plucked a string behind my ribs. The melody ripples through my bones, my muscles, my head.

I'm getting dizzy in that lung-aching way, like I've been underwater too long, like I need to come up for air. The woman's arm drifts up, and the next thing I know,

I'm moving *toward* her, making my way between the tombstones, toward her outstretched fingers, and—

"Cassidy!" Jacob cuts into my path. He takes my arm and pulls me back through the Veil. I fall through an instant of ice-cold air before landing on my butt in the grass.

"What was that for?" I ask.

"I kept calling you," he says. "You didn't answer." He shakes his head. "You really shouldn't cross the Veil without me."

"I didn't mean to," I say. "It kind of sucked me in."

His face is a mix of confusion and concern. I look past him, but of course the woman in the red cloak is gone, erased along with the rest of the Veil. The graveyard around us is full of chattering tourists and the sound of church bells as the kirk chimes the hour.

I get to my feet, brushing grass from my jeans. "Where have you *been*?"

Jacob ducks his head. "Sorry. I guess I . . . got a little lost . . ."

I think back to the mirror, the blank expression that

followed him out of the bedroom. Jacob shudders, as if not wanting to remember, so I try to forget.

"Did you see her?" I ask.

"Who?"

My eyes drift back to the place where she stood. "A woman in a red cloak . . ."

"There you are!" Mom calls, heading toward me. "I've been looking everywhere." She squints up at the sky. "I think you might be right about the rain. Ready to go?"

"You have no idea," I say, right before the first drops begin to fall.

By the time we get back to the Lane's End, Jacob is the only one still dry. We had an umbrella, but now it hangs from Mom's hand, a mangled mess, thin metal arms snapped and broken by the first strong gust of wind. Mom doesn't seem the least bit fazed, but water drips into my eyes and sloshes in my shoes as we mount the front steps, my jacket wrapped tightly over my camera.

Mom heads off to talk to Mrs. Weathershire, but Jacob and I continue up the broad wooden stairs. All I want is a hot shower and some dry clothes. The image of the beach house comes to mind, sudden and taunting.

"What was she like?" asks Jacob. "This woman in red."

I shake my head, trying to remember. But the pieces in my mind don't add up to what I saw. What I felt.

"I don't know," I say slowly. "But she wasn't like the other ghosts. She was too bright, too real, she didn't blend in, and when she saw me, she *saw* me, like, really saw—"

"Who are you talking to?"

The question comes out of nowhere. That is, until I climb the last few steps and see the girl from earlier. She's sitting primly in the window seat on the second-floor landing, a book open in her lap and her dark braid draped over one shoulder.

"Well?" she presses. Her accent is proper, so crisp I can't tell if she's actually a year or two older than me, or just *really* British. "Who were you talking to just now?"

"Myself," I say, trying not to cheat a glance at Jacob. "Don't you ever talk to yourself?"

She purses her lips. "I don't make a habit of it," she says, her gaze dropping back to her book.

"Come on, Cass," whispers Jacob. But that déjà vu sense is back, like the *tap-tap-tap* of the Veil, only this is a *tug*, pulling me closer.

"Are you staying here long?" I ask the girl.

"Who knows," she says, without looking up.

Okay, so, not the chattiest.

"Well, I should go change." I gesture at my clothes. "My pants are soaked."

A small sound escapes the girl's mouth, something between a snort and a scoff.

"You mean *trousers*."

I look at her blankly.

"Pants are . . . what you wear *underneath*."

Jacob cracks up at that, and it's crazy, but I swear the girl's gaze flicks toward him. Just for a second. It's so fast, I almost don't notice. So fast, I can't be sure. But Jacob goes quiet, and he moves to stand behind me.

"Biscuits, flats, lifts, trousers," I say. "I thought American people and British people spoke the same language."

"Hardly." She closes the book and gives me a sweeping look. "What brings *you* to Scotland?"

"Ghosts."

Her eyes narrow. "What do you mean?"

"My parents," I explain. "They're filming a show about famous ghosts around the world. This is our first stop."

The tension bleeds out of her face. "Ah. I see."

"Yeah," I say, "apparently Scotland is, like, *really* haunted."

"Apparently." She rises to her feet. That's when I notice the necklace.

It's a pendant on a long silver chain. As the girl straightens, the pendant spins. I realize it's not a pendant at all, but a small round mirror. It tickles something in the back of my head, but I don't know what. She's already tucking it beneath her collar.

"I'm Cassidy Blake," I say, thrusting out a hand.

She eyes me a moment before taking it. "Lara Jayne Chowdhury."

She starts past me down the stairs, and it's crazy, but I can *feel* her walking away, as if there's a rope spooling out between us. And maybe she can feel it, too, because she glances back and considers me a moment, forehead wrinkled in thought. "Do *you* believe in ghosts, Cassidy?"

I don't know how to answer that.

I mean, you're supposed to say no. But it's kind of hard to do that when Jacob's standing there, arms crossed, beside me. In the end, I guess my silence speaks for me, because Lara's mouth quirks into something like a smile.

"I'll take that as a yes," she says, vanishing down the stairs before I can ask what *she* believes.

Jacob waits until she's gone to speak.

"I've got a weird feeling about that girl," he says.

"Yeah," I say. "That makes two of us."

CHAPTER TEN

That night, Mom, Dad, and I sit on the floor around a low coffee table, eating takeaway fish and chips from a local shop. I'm skeptical about the idea of "fish and chips," but we passed six different places advertising this dish between the airport and the Lane's End, so there must be *something* to it.

I open the carton and stare down at the contents. A giant piece of fried fish sits on top of a sea of oversized French fries.

I look up, confused. "These aren't chips."

"Sure they are," says Mom with a devious grin, and I realize this is yet *another* one of those things that got lost in translation.

"Um, no," I insist. "These are *fries. Chips* come in a bag."

"Ah, here those kind of chips are called *crisps*."

It's official. Nothing is safe. I look around, peering under the stack of napkins. "What about ketchup?"

And at this point, Mom informs me that there is no ketchup, because the whole thing's been covered in *salt and vinegar*. The scent filling the room is a weird combo of fried food (good) and vinegar (a thing that I'm pretty sure does *not* go on food).

I'm about to rebel when Mom scoops up a chip/fry and holds it toward my face.

"Come on, Cass," she prompts, "just try it. If you hate it, we'll order pizza."

With my luck, *pizza* is the British word for *octopus*. I wrinkle my nose.

"Scaredy cat," teases Jacob from his place on the sofa, which isn't fair because it's not like *he* has to taste it.

I accept the thick "chip" from Mom and take a cautious bite.

My mouth fills with warm potato and salt, the bite of the vinegar weird but refreshing against the oil of the fries. It's unlike anything I've ever tasted.

And it's *totally delicious*.

I try the fish, and it's just as good. "Wow."

Mom beams. "See?"

"It's really good," I say, but the food is hot and my mouth is full so it comes out *isreagoo*.

"We'll have you eating haggis before the trip is done."

I have no idea what *that* is, but at the mention of it, even Dad cringes, so I decide not to ask. File it under: *Things better left a mystery.*

The chips, it turns out, are amazing as long as they're *hot*. The moment they get cold, they turn into a salty, soggy mess, which is what's happening to the contents of Dad's tray.

He hasn't touched his food. He's too busy poring over Mr. Weathershire's journals. They're a collection of accounts taken from neighbors, friends, fellow drinkers at the local pub.

"Fascinating," Dad murmurs. "The way they tie it all together, history and myth. You can see the pagan underpinnings and—"

"John," says Mom patiently. "Your dinner."

Dad makes a noncommittal sound and plucks a cold chip from the pile, popping it into his mouth. This is a pretty common sight at home: Dad, bent over his laptop, typing away while the remains of a meal sit forgotten to the side. Mom and I are used to it.

Jacob squints, narrowing all his focus on a soggy chip leaning halfway out of Dad's carton. If he were human, he'd probably have given himself a nosebleed by now, from all that concentrating. Instead, his whole body ripples from the effort as he reaches out and rests a finger on the chip. A second later it actually tips, and falls.

Jacob thrusts both arms into the air, the picture of triumph.

"Behold my telekinetic prowess!" he says, even though I'm pretty sure the chip was already losing its battle with gravity.

Dad turns the page of a weathered journal and *hmm*s to himself.

"Anything good?" I ask.

"It's a mix," he says. "Some are just ramblings and some are level-headed, but they all talk about these myths and legends as if they're fact."

Mom gives a triumphant smile. "Stories have power," she says. "So long as you believe them."

Dad nods absently. "Like here." He taps the page. "These are a series of stories about Burke and Hare."

The names sound familiar. Then I remember—I heard one of the street performers mention them on the Royal Mile.

"Who are they?" I ask, intrigued.

"Well, back in the early 1800s," Dad explains, "medical students needed bodies to practice on, and there was a shortage, so grave robbers would dig up the newly dead and deliver them to the medical theaters. But William Burke and William Hare decided that instead of digging up corpses, they would simply create their own."

Jacob shudders beside me.

I hold my breath.

"They murdered sixteen people before they were caught and tried. Hare testified against Burke and was eventually freed, but Burke was hanged, and then dissected in an anatomy theater, just as his victims had been."

Jacob and I exchange a horrified glance.

Dad turns the page. "According to this narrator, William Burke's bones are still in the university's medical school. His ghost haunts the halls, bringing with it the scent of death and grave dirt."

For a moment, none of us talk.

The wind picks up outside, an ominous whistling through the old window frame.

Dad flicks through the pages of the journal with his thumb.

"There are dozens of stories, some rooted in history, like Burke and Hare, others little more than urban legend. Plague victims buried in walls. Headless musicians. The ghost taverns. The Mackenzie poltergeist. The Raven in Red."

I sit up straight, remembering the woman in the Veil, the crimson of her cloak. My chest tightens.

"What's that one about?" I ask.

"Which one?"

"The Raven in Red."

Dad flips back a couple of pages. "Hmm. She shows up in a few different stories about missing children— I'm guessing she's a variant on the 'mourning mother' myth, the woman in widow's weeds who steals other children away. But there's no origin story, not in any of

Weathershire's journals. Now the plague vaults, that's a fascinating section . . ."

But I'm still stuck on *missing children.*

I can feel Jacob staring at me as my mind spins over the memory of the Veil, the woman's black hair and eyes, her hypnotic song. It's strange, but when I saw her, I wasn't afraid. On the contrary, she was like a patch of sun on a gray day. In that moment, when she sang, I *wanted* to follow her. I couldn't think of anything else.

But now that she's gone, the fear's caught up.

Mom claps her hands and pushes to her feet. "I think that's enough ghost stories for one night."

We clean up the remains of the fish and chips and get ready for bed. Dad shuts off the lights in the living room, and Jacob slips away, like he always does at night.

Ghosts don't need sleep, and after I found him once perched at the edge of my bed, watching *me* sleep, I told him that wasn't cool. Now I don't know *where* he goes—if he just turns off like a light or wanders the streets—I just know he's not here.

I can't stop yawning, and by the time I climb into my bed, I can feel myself sinking down into that murky place before sleep. The half-open window in my bedroom lets in a cool breeze and a wave of low, distant noise. Somewhere nearby, a baby cries. An old lady laughs. A couple fights.

At least, that's what it *sounds* like, at first, but I soon realize it's just seagulls, calling to each other in the dark. They squawk and trill and chatter, but the longer I listen, the more I think I can hear a woman's voice weaving through the wind, the highs and lows of her song dragging me down into sleep.

CHAPTER ELEVEN

The film crew turns up early the next morning, two men and a woman, all wearing black turtlenecks. They come bearing equipment, and fill our Lane's End flat with noise. They start discussing schedules, snapping atmosphere shots, turning the cozy living room into a whirlwind of technical talk.

Jacob gets whipped up by all the energy and starts playing his favorite game, which basically entails following around members of the crew, waving his hands in front of their faces and chatting as if he's a regular part of the fray.

I sit on the sofa, polishing raindrops off my camera lens and trying to stay out of the way. Grim lounges beneath the window and I snap a photo as he yawns, transforming for an instant into a tiny black lion.

"That's a great camera," says the woman on the film

crew. "Vintage." Her own camera hangs around her neck, massive and high-tech and full of settings. She notices Grim. "Oh, brilliant, is this the cat from the covers?" She kneels to grab a shot.

Jacob hops up beside the cat and strikes a pose, winking at me, and I laugh. We both know he won't show up on those fancy digital cameras—I can already see the picture on her screen—but it's fun, knowing there's more to the image than they will ever see.

I look down at my own camera. I don't have any way to see what I've shot, which means, until I get it developed, the film inside will stay a mystery, waiting to be exposed.

Mom and Dad appear, looking like they've stepped off the cover of one of their books: Dad in his tweed jacket, and Mom with her messy bun full of pens. I don't have a part to play. Apparently the network thought I'd add a "fun family element," but my parents were more protective, and that's fine with me—I've never loved performing, have always preferred being *behind* the camera. So I'm wrapped in a giant sweatshirt and leggings, watching while a man pins a tiny microphone to the inside of Dad's jacket. The woman pins a tiny microphone on Mom, who is busy arranging her folders.

Mom pulls out a sheet of paper with today's three filming locations:

1) *THE SOUTH BRIDGE VAULTS*
2) *MARY KING'S CLOSE*
3) *THE WHITE HART INN*

"Here, Cassidy," says Dad, handing me a cell phone, and I perk up. "This," he explains, "is yours. But data isn't cheap. This is for calls, and texts, and emergencies. *Not* Candy Crush." I roll my eyes.

A bright ringtone goes off, but it's not coming from my new phone. One of the crewmen announces that Findley's downstairs.

Findley, it turns out, is our official guide.

Mom, Dad, and I head downstairs (along with the crew and Jacob, of course). Findley is waiting for us in the sitting room. He's a stocky man with a trim beard and a bald patch in the middle of his red curls that makes it look like he's wearing a crown. He reminds me a little of a redheaded Hagrid.

Mrs. Weathershire is pouring him a cup of tea, the cup so small in his broad hand it looks like she's dumping hot water straight into his palm.

At the sight of our group, his face splits into a friendly smile.

"Findley Stewart," he introduces himself, eyes sparkling. "I hear you're looking for a fright. Well, you came to the right place." His booming voice has the cadence of those storytellers Mom and I passed on the Royal Mile.

Findley downs his tea in a single swallow and sets the cup aside. "Shall we?"

With that, we set out on foot, Findley in the lead.

"Wouldn't want to waste a patch of good weather," he says. "Around here," he explains, "you savor the sun whenever you get it—who knows how long it will last."

Findley and Mom seem to have the same definition of "good weather."

The ground is damp, and slivers of blue sky peek through the clouds, but they're quickly swallowed by gray.

Dad looks up, and as if on cue, a drop of rain hits his glasses. Findley smacks him on the back, laughs, and sets off down the road.

As we cross Old Town, Findley rambles on about plagues and murders, grave robbers and bodies buried in walls, as if talking about tea, cake, a nap in the sun.

Dad has his journal out, jotting down notes, his attention torn between writing details and not tripping on the cobblestone street. Mom's caught up in Findley's tales, leaning in like a sunflower to the light. I know from experience that Dad will handle the history, and Mom's job will be to paint the story. To make the viewer believe. She's good at it. She used to tell me stories so vivid I'd dream about them after. Or ones so scary I couldn't sleep.

It turns out Findley was friends with the late Mr. Weathershire. Findley used to go to pubs with him around the city, helped him collect those accounts that fill the dead man's journals. Findley seems to know a *lot* about the myths and legends of Edinburgh.

Which gives me an idea.

"Hey, Findley," I say. "Do *you* know the story of the Raven in Red?"

He rubs his head, thinking. "Och, aye," he says with a nod. "Been a long while since I've heard it . . ."

My heart speeds up.

"It's one of those you're raised with as a child," he goes on. "To keep you in your bed at night. Let me think . . . People tell it different ways—some say she lost a child, others that she couldn't have one, some that she was a widow, and others that she was a witch—but here's the version I know.

"Once there was a woman, a beauty with fair skin and black hair, and a little boy who loved to wander. And once there was a vicious winter, a snowstorm that turned the city white, and the boy went out to play and didn't come back. The woman put on the red cloak so her boy would see her, and went into the streets, and called for him, and sang for him, and cried for him, but he never came home. She searched all night, and all day, and she froze, or should have, but instead, something broke inside her. She began to set her sights on other children, began to call for them, and sing for them, and cry for them, until they came, drawn to her voice and her bright red cloak."

I meet Jacob's gaze, concern crossing his face.

"All winter, she stole children," continues Findley, "lured them away from warm beds and parents' arms and safe places. Their bodies were found outside her door, frozen on their feet."

I shiver at the thought. The memory of cold in my lungs. The idea of it climbing my skin. Encasing me in ice.

"But why do they call her the Raven?"

The question comes from Jacob, but I repeat it to Findley.

"Ah," says Findley, "perhaps for the birds that perch on her tombstone, or the color of her hair, or the way the story goes that if she catches you, the hand on your arm will turn to talons, and her voice will crack into a rasping *caw*, and her black hair will turn to wings, and she'll fly away with you in her grip. She haunts the city every winter, stealing children, feasting on their warmth."

"Like a pied piper?" prompts Mom.

"Aye, and nae," says Findley. "The piper's a fairy tale. Our Raven, she's a ghost. Hung for her crimes and buried in our own Greyfriars Kirk. New mothers leave baubles and bells on the grave," he adds. "Like a patron saint, only you pray for her to stay away." He breaks into a warm smile. "But you needn't worry about the Raven this time of year. She comes with the cold."

Then why, I wonder, did I see her in the graveyard? Why did she seem to want me?

Dad pushes his glasses up. "Do you believe in ghosts, then, Mr. Stewart?"

Findley strokes his beard. "I'll tell you what I believe in, Mr. Blake. I believe in history." Dad brightens. *Right answer*, I think. Findley goes on. "Edinburgh's got an awful lot of history, not all of it cheery. The kind of things my city's seen, well, it's bound to leave a mark. Now, whether that's a gravestone or a ghost, I can't tell you, but you'd be hard pressed to find someone who hasn't felt a spirit or seen a thing that makes them wonder."

We turn onto a broad street called South Bridge: the first stop on our filming schedule.

As we pass coffee shops and bookstores and a dozen other ordinary places, I begin to relax. I can feel the Veil, but it's not exactly tapping on my shoulder. Instead, the pull is softer, brushing against the soles of my shoes, as if wafting up from the street.

The crew members check their gear and start filming, while my parents narrate.

"South Bridge," starts Mom, "may look like an ordinary street, but the vaults nested *below* are the site of many hauntings."

Oh, come on, I think, looking down.

"Nope, nope, nope," says Jacob.

"Nineteen vaults, to be exact," says Dad. "And it was indeed a bridge," he adds, "before the city rose around it."

"Some say South Bridge was cursed from the start," Mom goes on. "When the bridge was first completed, the honor of crossing it fell to a judge's wife, but she died days before the ceremony . . ." Mom pauses in a doorway. "Torn between their superstitions and their plans, the city decided to mark the bridge's opening by sending her coffin instead."

"Cut," says one of the crew. "That's great."

"Our permit here's for tomorrow," says another, "so we'll wait until then to film the vaults."

Jacob and I both sigh in relief.

We turn at the corner, and we're back on the Royal Mile, with its street performers and tour guides in old-fashioned clothes.

The crew films what Findley calls "B roll" of Mom and Dad walking through the crowd, framed by the grand old buildings. Then Findley leads us to a small shop. The sign outside reads THE REAL MARY KING'S CLOSE. "What's a *close*?" I ask.

"A *close*," explains Dad, "is a cluster of lanes and alleys where people used to work and live. But as the city spread, the new grew up over the old, and the lanes were buried. The underground streets were forgotten for centuries. And then they were found."

"That sounds promising," deadpans Jacob as we step inside.

Where I'm surprised to find, of all things, a *gift shop*.

There are these tall wire racks that hold souvenirs and pamphlets, and blown-up photos on the wall, and a counter where you buy tickets, and none of it seems particularly scary.

"Ah, the television crew," says a woman behind the counter.

"We've been expecting you," adds a male colleague brightly.

The woman rounds the counter and waves us toward a second set of doors. "We can give you an hour," she says, opening the door.

A cool draft billows through it, and a bad feeling wells in my chest.

Mom glances at me. "Sweetheart," she says. "You don't have to come down with us if you don't want to."

"Did you hear that?" says Jacob. "We could just stay up here, where everything's nice and not as haunted."

But there it is again, that *tap-tap-tap*. The urge to turn around and peel back the curtain.

I square my shoulders. "No," I say. "I'm coming with."

Jacob groans, and Findley grins. "There's our girl."

The crew passes out what they call "torches"—apparently the British word for *flashlights*. Armed with the dull electric glow, we make our way down into the dark.

CHAPTER TWELVE

As we descend, so does the temperature.

It drops a little with every step. Only there are no steps, because the entrance to Mary King's Close is like a set of stairs filed smooth. A downward slope lit only by dull yellow bulbs on the walls.

Sheets hang on clotheslines overhead, and it's hard to believe that we're underground, even with the damp air and smell of old earth, wet stone.

But soon, the ground levels out. We reach the bottom of the slope.

"That wasn't so bad," I say.

Findley laughs. "Oh, lass, that wasn't the Close." He takes my shoulder and turns me to the right. "*This* is the Close."

Oh.

It sprawls before me: a maze of narrow streets and

covered doorways, stone arches and places where the light doesn't reach. I hear the distant drip of water, and see shadows dancing on the walls.

Jacob crosses his arms over his T-shirt. "Well, this is just great."

The camera crew sets up, testing their equipment and adjusting their lights.

"Almost forgot," says Findley. He hands Mom a small rectangular device. It looks like a walkie-talkie with a row of lights across the front.

"An EMF meter!" Mom squeaks, delighted. Her voice echoes through the tunnels as she waves the device at me. "Electromagnetic field," she explains. "To measure paranormal activity."

She flips the switch, and the meter emits a faint hiss, like the sound of a radio between stations. Mom swings it back and forth, as if searching for a signal. Jacob shoots me a mischievous glance and takes a step toward it. The device comes to life, emitting a low tone.

"What do you know?" Mom says. "It works."

I think of telling her that it's Jacob, but the last thing

I need is for the show's crew to know my best friend is a ghost. Still . . . I have to admit, it's pretty cool, seeing his presence register on the device.

Jacob steps back, and the sound dies away, leaving only the drip of water on stone, the shuffle of our feet.

It's quiet down here, but not as quiet as it should be.

The wind whistles, and I think I hear someone calling, the words just out of reach. When Findley catches me straining to hear, he smiles.

"It's just the old city playing tricks," he whispers.

"Or is it?" says Mom with a wink. And then she turns to the camera, and the filming starts.

"The trouble with Mary King's Close," Mom begins, "goes back to the plague."

"When it comes to corpses," offers Dad in his teacher's tone, "there are two great sources in history: sickness and war."

"And Scotland's had plenty of both," adds Mom.

Dad picks up, the story passed between them like a relay baton. "When the plague came to Edinburgh and people fell sick, the healthy were so afraid of the ill that sometimes they buried them *before* they were dead."

I shudder and look at Jacob, and he looks back, blue eyes wide in mock horror. Or maybe real horror. It's hard to tell when Jacob's *actually* scared and when he's just humoring me.

This is how it is between us.

He pretends to be scared, even when he's not.

I pretend *not* to be scared, even when I am.

I move closer to him. Even though Jacob's not flesh and blood, I feel better next to him. We stand edge to edge, as close as we can without me putting an elbow through his side.

The Veil taps on my shoulder, and my fingers tighten reflexively on my camera strap.

"Don't even think about it," warns Jacob.

Don't worry, I think back.

The Veil dances at the edge of my sight, trying to tempt me to turn and look, but I don't. There's a darkness to it here, a *malice*, like the energy in Greyfriars Kirk.

"How do you make a ghost?" asks Mom. She's speaking softly now, as if she's sitting on the edge of my bed. "Maybe it's how a person lived. But I've always believed it's how they *died*." She raps her knuckles on the nearest wall. "There's a reason we call these spirits *restless*."

This isn't at *all* like those cheesy ghost shows on TV. The way my parents speak . . . it's like Mom is reading a story out loud. Like Dad's lecturing at the front of his class. They're naturals, and I'm so drawn in by their voices that for a few minutes, I forget to be afraid. Forget that we're standing in a buried maze, surrounded by bones.

And then I glance sideways and find a pair of eyes staring out at me from a pale face.

I yelp, knocking backward into Findley.

"Cut," calls one of the cameramen.

"Sorry," I mumble, feeling guilty for ruining the take. "I saw . . ."

The second cameraman swings his light into the shadows. It glances off the plastic sheen of a wax figure.

"Oh," says Findley. "Those are all over this place. For *ambiance*."

"That's perfectly normal," says Jacob dryly. "Not messed up at all."

Mom and Dad, the film crew, and Findley head down a hall. When I start to follow them, the *tap-tap-tap* weakens a little. I turn and survey the corridor, taking a step in another direction. The Veil gets stronger. If this were a game of Hot and Cold, I'd be getting warmer while my parents head straight into icy water.

Mom and Dad may be brilliant, but they clearly don't know a thing about finding *actual* ghosts.

I wait until they're between takes—the little red camera lights safely off—before calling out, "This way."

This way way way, my voice echoes.

Mom and Dad double back, the crew trailing behind them.

"Find something?" asks Findley.

I shrug. "Just a feeling."

We move through a low doorway. The world closes in, the ceiling falling to just above Dad's head. A narrow room. No windows. All stone.

It reminds me of a tomb.

The cameras start rolling. And the EMF meter goes off again.

But this time, Jacob's nowhere near it. The volume shifts from the low tone it made before to a high whine, practically a wail.

"Well, this is a whole lot of nope," says Jacob, backing away.

Don't you dare leave me here, I hiss in my head.

I've never been that claustrophobic, but I'm starting to wish I'd stayed street-side. While Mom and Dad are filming, I retreat into the hall, and I don't notice the *tap-tap-tap* rushing up behind me until it's too late.

The Veil reaches out.

"When the lower streets were bricked over during the plague . . ." says Dad.

It grabs at my shoulders.

". . . some of the victims were buried inside . . ."

It clutches at my sleeves.

"Cass," warns Jacob as I squeeze my eyes shut.

I *won't* turn around.

I *won't* look.

I *won't*—

But in the end it doesn't matter.

The Veil parts behind me, and I gasp, cold air flooding my lungs as I'm dragged under.

*   *   *

Mary King's Close is *full* of ghosts.

They cough, call out, shuffle past. Someone lets out a hacking sound. A bundle of rags on the ground rolls over. There's a person—*was* a person—in there.

Bricks are piled on the damp ground, and half-built walls rise and fall to every side. Somewhere nearby, a fist pounds dully on stone.

Jacob groans and runs a hand through his messy blond hair. "*Cass.*"

"I didn't mean to," I say.

"I know," he answers, crossing his arms over his chest with a shiver. "Let's just get out of here."

I look around.

The film crew and Findley and my parents have disappeared, swept behind the curtain. If I strain, I can still hear them, their voices ghostly, echoing. But when I reach for the Veil, my hand finds something too solid. More like a wall than a curtain.

That's not good. I try to swallow the rising panic as a skeletal man hobbles past.

An old woman sobs.

A family huddles together for warmth.

Jacob inches closer to me, the air around us thick with fear and loss and illness.

A ripple moves through the ghosts, their heads turning as they notice me. An intruder in their deaths, their memories, their world.

The skeletal man stops walking.

The old woman narrows her milky eyes.

The family glares.

"Cassidy," whispers Jacob. I reach for the Veil, hoping to catch the part in the curtain and cross back through, but it holds firm under my touch. I keep trying. This has never happened before.

The ghosts are moving now.

Toward us.

"Jacob," I say slowly, trying to keep the panic out of my voice. "A little help?"

"Stay calm," he says. "I'll get us out of here." He puts his hand on my arm and I can feel the bones in his fingers as his grip tightens.

Still, nothing happens.

"Jacob?"

He grunts, like he's trying to lift something heavy.

I can tell he's trying to pull us back through the Veil, only it's definitely not working, because we're still here, and the ghosts are still coming toward us, bringing with them a wave of

Menace.

Malice.

Anger.

Terror.

Sickness.

Sorrow.

It feels like ice water in my lungs, like aching cold in my bones. I can't peel the two apart. Can't separate my memories from theirs, what I once felt from what they do now, over and over.

"Jacob!" I gasp, breathless.

"I'm trying!"

I inch back until I'm standing against the wall. My hands fumble for the camera at my neck, clinging to it like a talisman, a reminder of what's real. My fingers brush one of the buttons—

And the flash goes off.

A flare of light bursts from my hands, a sudden, dazzling slash of white in the darkened tunnels.

The ghosts draw back, some shielding their eyes, others blinking, as if blinded. It won't last. But in that stolen second, Jacob grabs my hand and pulls me through a gap in the line of ghosts, and we run.

CHAPTER THIRTEEN

We bolt through the maze of underground alleys. I can feel the ghosts behind us, hear them coming, but I don't look back, feet carrying me over rough stone, through doorways and rooms and down corridors.

At last, I spot a set of stairs.

Up. That's all I can think. Up. Every step takes us farther from Mary King's Close and its ghostly mob and that horrible wave of feelings.

Halfway to the street, the Veil thins enough for me to reach out and grab the curtain—which is finally cloth again—and force it aside. We tumble through, out of the Veil and back into a world of pale light and fresh air.

I gasp at the cold in my lungs, the sense of surging up from deep water. The weight of Jacob's hand is gone, but he's still there beside me. Sunlight filters through him as he leans back against the alley wall.

I look around, lost.

No, not *lost*—it's hard to get lost when you can hear the noise of the Royal Mile in the distance. Plus, the ground slopes beneath me, so that *up* leads to one place, and *down* to another. I'm not lost—but I don't know where I am, either.

I was so focused on getting out of Mary King's Close, out of the Veil, that I didn't exactly pay attention to the route. I must have taken a different set of stairs, because Jacob and I are standing on a narrow street I've never seen before. It's three parts gray stone to one part gray sky. There's no bustle, no noise.

I slump back against the wall and slide down until I'm sitting on the ground, which is probably unsanitary, but I don't care. My skin still feels like it's coated in cobwebs and every time I blink, I see the ghosts. The way they looked at me, with their want and their anger and their fear.

I've been in plenty of haunted places, but I've never been to a place where the Veil was stronger than I am. Stronger than *Jacob*. He's standing over me, arms crossed, and I wish for once I could read his mind because I can't read his face.

"We should have just gone for a walk in the city," I say at last.

He sighs and crouches down beside me. "Makes you miss creepy students in burning auditoriums, doesn't it?"

I try to smile. We sit for a moment, quiet except for the seagulls overhead and the faraway sound of bagpipes.

"You okay?" Jacob asks, which I appreciate. He knows I'm not, but he still asks, and I know that if I lie, he won't call me out on it. We'll just pretend—that we're normal, that he's not a mind-reading ghost, that I'm not . . . whatever I am. That I'm not drawn toward places full of death like a rock rolling down a hill. Constant as gravity.

What's wrong with me?

"Where should I start?" he teases.

I shoulder him, feel a prickle of cold as my arm goes straight through his sleeve.

"That tickles," he says, getting up. He holds out his hand and I wish I could take it. Instead, I push off the wall. I'm halfway to my feet when Jacob glances to his right and says, "No way."

I follow his gaze and see a girl crossing the road.

I recognize her instantly. The brown skin, the black hair pulled back in a neat braid. The girl from the Lane's End.

Lara Jayne Chowdhury.

As she walks, she holds her necklace in one hand, the mirror pendant spinning in her fingers, catching the light.

"What is she doing?" wonders Jacob as Lara slips around a corner.

"No idea," I say, straightening up. "But I want to find out."

We follow her, rounding the corner just in time to see Lara stop, glance left and right, and then *disappear.*

Right out of the street—and into nothing.

Which isn't possible.

"Unless . . ." starts Jacob.

I finish for him. *Unless she's like me.*

I remember the feeling of recognition. The way Lara looked at me and seemed to hear Jacob when he laughed.

Do you believe in ghosts? she'd asked me.

I cross to the spot where she vanished, and can feel the ripple of the curtain as it settles back into place.

Lara didn't step into nothing.

She stepped into the *Veil*.

And I'm already reaching out for it when Jacob cuts in front of me.

"No," he says. "Did you forget what just happened? Did you forget the part where we got *stuck*?"

"Of course not," I say, the memory of the ghosts still fresh. But I've never met someone like me. I have to see. Have to know. I catch hold of the curtain, pulling it aside.

"You can stay here," I tell Jacob, and for a second, I think he's really going to, as if he can't hear my thoughts pounding with my pulse.

You can stay, but I don't want you to.

Jacob huffs. "Rule number nine," he grumbles, following me through.

The Veil is thinner here, the transition easy. The chill in my lungs is barely a breath, a shiver, and then it's gone.

We pass through. My feet land on old stone streets.

The light shines from my chest. Beside me, Jacob is solid—and solidly ticked off.

He gestures around at the alley. "Well?"

It's empty. No Lara. No ghosts. Nothing but a thin mist.

But that's not possible. I saw her disappear. I saw—

A familiar English-accented voice cuts through the silence. "Watch and listen . . ."

The words carry on the air, and when I follow them around the nearest corner, I see Lara standing at the bottom of a short set of steps. Her back is to us, and she's grayed out, the same way I am, with the same burning light inside her chest.

And there, sprawled back against the stairs, as if trying to escape, is a ghost. A man my father's age. He's got a short beard and a long coat that pools around him like a shadow.

Lara's necklace dangles from her outstretched hand, mirror side hanging in front of the ghost like a hypnotist's pendulum. Only, it's not swinging side to side. It's not moving at all. It stays perfectly still, and so does the man.

Jacob's gone rigid beside me. I hold my breath.

"See and know . . ." continues Lara.

The words sound almost like a spell. Maybe they *are* a spell, because the ghost stays there on the steps, as if pinned. Lara stands tall, fingers splayed as she recites the third and final line.

"This is what you are."

The air ripples with the force of the words, the whole Veil shuddering. As I watch, the ghost goes thin, like glass and fog instead of flesh and bone. I can see straight through him, can see the thing coiled in his chest. A coil of rope, a ribbon.

Like mine, but without light.

Lara reaches in and pulls the ribbon out. The end snags in his chest, but she gives it a swift tug. The dark thread comes free in her hand, hanging limply from her fingers for a moment before crumbling away to ash.

An instant later, the man crumbles, too, just . . . falls apart. One second a ghost, and the next gone. A breeze sweeps through the alley, sudden and unnatural, and blows the dust away.

Jacob lets out a small gasp, and Lara's head snaps up.

I shove Jacob sideways behind the corner and out of sight as she turns, brushing the last bits of dust from her hands.

I stare in shock.

She gives me a long, measured look, her brown eyes unblinking.

"What?" she says at last. "You act like you've never seen a ghost hunter before."

PART THREE

GHOST HUNTERS

CHAPTER FOURTEEN

hat do you . . ." I trail off, unsure what to say.

A *ghost hunter?* At the edge of my sight, Jacob shudders, and I'm suddenly glad she can't see him.

"I should have known," she goes on matter-of-factly.

"Known what?"

"That you were like me." She loops the necklace back over her head, tucking the pendant underneath her shirt. I notice that the light in *her* chest is a warmer hue, rose-tinted, while mine is bluer, colder. "I suppose I suspected, back at the Lane's End. But you seemed so very clueless. Almost like you do right now—"

"Hey." I bristle. "I knew there was something weird about you, too."

She arches a perfect black brow. "Really, now?"

"I just didn't know what it was," I explain. "I didn't realize there were other people . . . who could . . ."

"Oh," she says, adjusting her braid. "You thought you were the only one who's ever cheated death? The only one able to move through the in-between? How novel."

"In-between?"

She gestures around us.

"Oh," I say, "the Veil."

Lara raises a brow. "That's what you call this place?"

"It's better than *in-between*," I shoot back. Lara starts to protest when we're cut off by voices, footsteps, the nearness of new ghosts. Plural. Lara and I both stiffen.

"We shouldn't stay here," she says, turning on her heel and vanishing back through the Veil without a second glance. I'm about to go after her, when Jacob catches my wrist.

"I don't like this," he hisses. "I don't like her. Did you see what she *did* to that guy? Because I did, Cass. She turned him to *ash*."

I know. I saw. But my head is spinning with questions.

Maybe Lara has answers. I pull free of Jacob's grip

and step through the Veil. There's a flush of cold, and then I'm back on the solid side of things.

Jacob didn't follow me through.

Lara pinches the bridge of her nose. "Edinburgh gives me a headache."

"What did you—" I start.

"I thought the in-between back in London was bad, but there's something about this city, can't you feel it? Like a lead blanket—"

"What did you *do* to him?" I ask.

Her eyes flick up. "To who?"

"The man on the steps."

She crinkles her nose. "He wasn't a *man*," she says primly. "He was a *ghost*. I sent him on."

"Where?"

She shrugs. "To the great unknown? To the silent side? To peace and quiet? Call it what you like. I sent him to the place *beyond*. Where he's *supposed to be*."

Supposed to be? "Why?"

Lara's eyebrows go up. "Excuse me?"

"Why did you do it?"

She bristles. "Because it's my *job*."

"Someone hired you to hunt ghosts?"

"Of course not," she says. "But this is what we *do*."

We? Hunt ghosts? I don't understand. And I must have said so out loud because Lara sighs and says, "Obviously. Ghosts don't stay in the in-between because they want to be there, Cassidy. They stay because they can't move on. They're stuck. It's up to us to set them free."

Us.

She frowns. "What have you been *doing* in your *Veil*, if not hunting ghosts?" Her eyes go to the camera around my neck. "Oh god, tell me you're not *sightseeing*!"

"Um . . ." My mouth opens, closes. I don't know what to say.

Her phone chimes with a text message, and she checks it. "Ugh, I have to go."

"Wait," I manage, "you can't just *leave*."

"I'm already late," she says, starting up the alley. "I'm supposed to meet Aunt Alice at the museum. Mum and Dad insist on weekly bouts of *cultural enrichment* or some such . . . Oh," she adds, almost as an afterthought. "You do know you're being haunted, right? A boy," she continues, holding up her hand, "about this tall, scruffy blond hair, bull's-eye shirt . . ."

I stiffen. No one else has ever been able to see Jacob.

"Yes," I say carefully. "I know."

Lara frowns. "And you haven't done anything about it?"

And there's a rock in my stomach, because I know what she means by that. It's in the job title: *ghost hunter.* "He's my *friend.*"

She purses her lips as if tasting something sour. "Bad idea." She looks like she's about to say more, but her cell phone dings again, and she just shakes her head and walks briskly toward the mouth of the alley.

"Wait," I say. "Please, I've never met anyone else who's . . . who can . . . you said . . ."

A dozen questions tumble through my head, and she must be able to see them because she says, "I'm in 1A."

"Huh?"

"My flat, at the Lane's End. Come by tomorrow morning. Ten o'clock." She steps out onto the street. "Don't be late."

*   *   *

I slump back against the wall, mind racing.

This is what we do.

My job . . . to hunt ghosts . . . to send them on . . . Is that why I'm able to cross the Veil?

And an even more unsettling question: Does Jacob *know*?

Has he always known?

As if on cue, Jacob reappears. Rises right up through the cobblestones, his arms crossed and his eyes dark. I can tell he's not happy.

I try to push all the questions from my head so he can't hear them, but it's like he's not even listening.

"Did you have a nice chat?" he asks coldly.

"Don't be like that," I say. "I was just curious. I didn't know there were other people who could cross the Veil. Did *you*?"

He scuffs the ground with his sneaker. "No."

He clearly doesn't want to talk anymore, but I can't stop the other questions from bubbling up. "Did you know what I really was, Jacob? What I could do?"

He winces but says nothing.

"You said there were rules to the Veil."

"There *are*."

"Ones you couldn't tell me. Was *that* true? Or did you just not want to?"

Jacob reddens and looks away, and it's as good as an answer.

"You didn't trust me," I say, surprised how much it hurts to put into words.

Jacob shakes his head. "It's not like that, Cass."

"Rule number six of friendship, Jacob. Friends don't leave friends in the dark."

He looks pained. "I'm sorry. I was just"—he shakes his head—"afraid . . ."

"Of what?" I ask, but before he can answer, my for-emergencies-only phone goes off in my pocket.

Uh-oh.

"*Cassidy?*" says Dad, sounding really worried when I answer. "Where are you?"

"Sorry," I say quickly. "I needed some air, and then I got turned around."

I follow Dad's instructions, Jacob on my heels, until we get back to the mouth of Mary King's Close. Dad appears a second later, his hair mussed and his glasses dusty.

"There you are," he says. "We've been looking *everywhere*. I called your phone four times before you answered."

Apparently there's no cell reception in the Veil.

Dad turns and calls back down the tunnel. "I found her!"

Found her, found her, found her, echoes away.

"Sorry," I say, ducking my head. "I guess I got a little spooked."

Dad pulls me in for a hug. "Can I tell you a secret?" I nod, and he says, "This place gives me the creeps, too." He squeezes my shoulder. "But don't tell your mother," he adds. "I've got a reputation to maintain."

Mom shows up a few moments later, the camera crew and Findley in tow.

"That was brilliant!" she says, cheeks flushed. Leave it to Mom to love a good scare. I bet she'd love it even more if she could see the other side. Dad shoots her a look and she sobers, her grin replaced by a very parental frown. "Except for the part where you disappeared, young lady. That was decidedly *not* brilliant."

I mumble a half-hearted apology.

Findley winks at me. "Have we made a believer of you yet?"

"Oh," says Mom, "Cassidy's always been a believer."

Findley's rusty eyebrows go up. "That so?" he asks with newfound respect.

"Her best friend is a spirit."

And just like that, she takes me from interesting to crazy.

"*Mom.*" I glare at her.

She throws her arms around me. "Embrace your strange, dear daughter. Where's the fun in being normal?"

Spoken like someone who doesn't see ghosts.

CHAPTER FIFTEEN

We end the day in a place called Grassmarket.

Of course, there's no grass, and I don't see any signs of a market. Just a wide-open plaza surrounded by shops and pubs. The castle looms behind the buildings like an eerie sentinel, but the plaza itself is nice, airy, open.

This isn't so bad, I think, right before Mom tells me that it used to be an execution ground. Why am I even surprised?

Sure enough, as we follow the crew across the square, the Veil thickens around my arms and legs until it feels like I'm walking through water. The only reason I don't get pulled in is because my mind is still stuck on Lara Chowdhury: her mirror necklace, her strange incantation, and the way the ghost fell apart at her feet.

This is what we do.

Jacob fidgets nervously beside me. We haven't talked

any more about what happened in the alley, about what he meant when he said he was afraid to tell me, but now's not the time. So we do our best to pretend that nothing's wrong.

Dad gestures to a low stone slab, a marker on the ground. "See that, Cassidy? Hundreds were put to death right here." The Veil turns leaden as I reach out to run my hand along the marker.

"Haha noooo," says Jacob, shooing me away.

By the time we reach the final stop on our filming list—a pub called the White Hart Inn, supposedly known for its hauntings—I'm prepared for the worst. So I'm relieved when the *tap-tap-tap* of the Veil fades to a distant prickle.

Mercifully, this pub isn't haunted.

At least, no more haunted than the rest of the city. Which is good, because I've officially had my fair share of all things *Inspecters* for one day. Mom and Dad and the crew head to the back of the pub to film, while Findley and I (and Jacob) slide into a corner booth and order food.

Findley gets up to go to the bar, but while he's gone, Jacob and I don't talk. I can't stop myself from thinking about what he said—and didn't say. Jacob keeps his eyes pointedly on the table, trying to lift a coaster from the wood.

At last, Findley reappears, setting down two pints of beer.

"Um," I say, "I'm not exactly old enough to drink."

He laughs, a low, rich bellow. "S'not for you," he says. He pulls one glass toward him. "This one's mine . . ." he explains, nudging the other toward the empty seat at his side, "and this one's Reggie's."

I look around the pub. "Reggie?"

"Reggie Weathershire," says Findley. "My old mate. This was his favorite place."

My eyes widen. Mrs. Weathershire's late husband. The one who's been dead for eight years.

"Do you think he's haunting here?" I ask.

Findley gives an amicable shrug. "Couldn't say. But if he is, I don't want him to go thirsty. I always bought the first round."

There's no sign of Mr. Weathershire, not on this side of the Veil. But Dad once told me that the living hold on to the dead, that "ghosts" are just our way of keeping people with us. Of course, I know there's more to it than that, but the thought of Mr. Weathershire being there in the pub seems to make Findley happy.

A big basket of fries—I mean chips—comes to the table. I douse them in vinegar and pop one into my mouth.

Findley chuckles. "We'll make a local of you yet."

I reach for another chip. "Do you *really* believe in ghosts?"

"Aye," he says without a second's pause. "In a sense. I believe there's something left behind when a person goes, a kind of memory. I've lived too long in this city not to believe it. But I don't think they really mean us harm."

Lara would probably disagree with that.

"And even if they do . . ." he adds, "I hear you've got your own ghost for a guardian angel." I tense, but there's no teasing in his voice. There's a mischievous light in his eyes, but he's not mocking me. "You've nothing to fear with a friend like that."

Jacob looks up, smiles tightly. "You know I've always got your back, Cass."

"So," says Findley, "tell me about this ghost of yours. What's his name?"

I pop another chip into my mouth. "Jacob," I say. "He saved my life," I add.

Findley's eyebrows go up. "Did he, now? Well, aren't you lucky."

I cut a glance at Jacob. *I am.*

Jacob blushes and looks down at the table. Shortly after, Mom and Dad turn up with the crew, and the rest of the meal is a lot of technical talk about the show. I stack towers of chips. Jacob tries to knock them down.

When it's time to go, we all haul ourselves up, equipment and all, and head for the doors. I glance back at the table one last time and see that Mr. Weathershire's glass is empty.

If this day has taught me anything, it's that I've still got a lot to learn.

Maybe the world is even stranger than I know.

The camera crew says good night and the rest of us make our way back to the Lane's End. Dad and Findley are deep in conversation, Jacob is whistling the theme song of some cartoon I can't place, and Mom has her head tipped back to enjoy the summer air. The moon is high.

The night is crisp and clear and perfect, and I snap photos of the winding streets, the amber streetlights. Even though I'm not in the Veil, there really is something magical about this city.

We're at the top of the Royal Mile when I hear the song.

It echoes up the road, and at first I think it's coming from a street performer or a bagpiper. But the street is empty, dark. And the sound is crystal clear.

It is a woman singing.

Her voice snags in my head like a hook, slowing my steps. I know that song. Or rather, I know the voice of the person singing it. Because it's not a person at all. I can picture her red cloak, her black curls, her out-stretched hand. I stop walking and turn in a circle, searching for the song. It's so close. I want to find it.

I *need* to find it.

"Do you hear that?" I whisper. But no one else seems to notice the singing, not even Jacob, who looks at me like I've lost my mind. I crane my head, listen, listen, but before I can find the source of the melody, it's gone.

I don't hear anything but wind.

* * *

Mom and Dad stay up late, going over the day's footage and preparing for tomorrow's filming. I, meanwhile, head straight to bed; all I want to do is sleep (and preferably dream about something other than haunted alleys and buried crypts).

But sleep doesn't come.

Doesn't stick.

I end up tossing and turning. When I close my eyes, I see the broken tunnels of Mary King's Close, the way a dozen sickly faces turned toward me. The scene dissolves, and I'm aboveground, Lara Chowdhury standing in the street, the mirror pendant hanging from her fingers.

Watch and listen . . .

See and know . . .

This is what you are . . .

It's the middle of the night when I throw off the covers and get up, nearly tripping on Grim. I slip out into the living room. The door to my parents' room is ajar, but the lights are out, and I can hear Dad snoring softly.

"Jacob?" I whisper, hoping he's nearby, but there's no answer.

I cross to the old-fashioned desk beneath the window. My camera sits on its purple strap in a pool of moonlight. I pick it up, look at the counter on top—I've got ten pictures left on the reel. I turn the device over in my hands, intending to clean off the lens with the cuff of my pajama shirt, when I spot something.

I'm not usually on this side of the camera, so I never noticed the way the lens reflects, like a piece of glass. Or a *mirror*.

Is this why Jacob never looks at the camera when I take his picture?

How many secrets is he keeping?

How many things do I still have to figure out?

CHAPTER SIXTEEN

"A re you sure you don't want to come?" Mom asks me the next morning. "We're going to explore the vaults beneath South Bridge. It's supposed to be positively *brimming* with paranormal activity."

Is this how normal parents speak to their children?

"Since when is anything about your family normal?" says Jacob.

"I'm sure," I tell Mom, pulling Grim close. "I think I'll sit this one out."

"Is everything all right?" asks Dad, scrawling a few last-minute thoughts in his notebook.

"Yeah," I say. I *don't* say there's a girl downstairs waiting to talk to me about hunting ghosts. I don't let myself even think it, not with Jacob there, and the secret hanging between us like a lie. Instead, I take the tried-and-trusty angle of fear. "It's just . . ." I bite my lip for effect. "I'm still kind of freaked out from Mary King's

Close . . ." It *was* pretty scary. And there's that whole part where the Veil *wouldn't let me go*. "I'm not sure I'm ready to do it again."

"Oh, honey," says Mom, brushing the hair from my face. "I heard you tossing and turning last night. Was that why?" I nod, and she pats my head. "You've always been so sensitive to those things."

"Drowning didn't help," offers Jacob cheerfully. I shoot him a warning look.

"The energy down there," I say with a shiver, "it was just *so dark*."

Jacob snorts. He clearly thinks I'm laying it on a little thick, but Mom nods sympathetically. "There was definitely something malevolent down there," she says.

"Perhaps," says Dad, "it wasn't the best place to take a child."

I almost bristle at that. I hate when they call me a *child*. And I can tell by his tone that he and Mom have had this talk before. That Dad didn't think I should have come to Edinburgh in the first place. Was there a version of this story without me in it?

"No!" I blurt out. "I'll be fine. I just need a day. Not

even a day. A morning! A few normal hours without spirits or specters or poltergeists or ghosts or . . ." I'm rambling now. Jacob frowns, and I can tell he's trying to figure out what on earth I'm thinking, but I focus on my parents. "It was probably the combination of greasy food and jet lag. I'll get my ghost-finding feet under me," I finish assuredly.

"I'm sure you will," says Mom. She kisses me on the head.

Dad leaves me some cash for emergencies, as well as their filming schedule for the day and strict instructions to stay put in the Lane's End until they get back, because Edinburgh may be a very pretty city, but it's still a foreign one.

"Have fun chasing ghosts," I call out as the door swings shut behind them.

Jacob flops onto the couch beside me. "What should we do now?" he wonders aloud. "We can watch weird Scottish television, or see where Mrs. Weathershire hides the biscuits, or . . . Why are you looking at me like that?"

"Don't freak out," I say slowly.

His eyes narrow. "That's really not the way to start a sentence if you want me to stay calm."

I fidget, but there's no use lying to him. Lying is hard enough. Lying to someone who can read your mind is nearly impossible.

"I kind of need to see someone."

Jacob doesn't have to ask me who. He can see the answer, plastered across my thoughts, and I can see his horror, plastered across his face.

"You've got to be kidding me."

"We're just going to talk."

"I can't *believe* you're going to see her!"

I don't want to fight with Jacob again. Not about this. He can't be mad at me for wanting to *understand*—

"She's a *ghost hunter*," he says, gesturing down at himself. "You know, someone who *hunts ghosts*."

"I know what she is. But for the last year, I thought I was the only one who could cross the Veil. I'm sorry if I'm curious, but I've never met anyone else like me."

"But she's *not* like you!" he snaps. "You take pictures of ghosts. You don't"—he waves his hand—"you don't *unmake* them."

But that's the problem. What if I'm *supposed* to?

Jacob must hear me think it, because his face contorts. I've never seen Jacob this mad before. Anger changes people, but it changes ghosts even more. His edges ripple and the color goes out of his face. He looks ... ghoulish.

"I'm all for you making friends, Cass," he says, and I want to tell him I doubt Lara is interested in friendship, but he doesn't give me a chance, "but maybe you could choose someone who doesn't turn people like *me* to dust."

Before I can stop myself, I shoot back, "If you'd been honest with me from the start, maybe I wouldn't have to go looking for answers somewhere else!"

Jacob glares at me long and hard, then throws up his hands and vanishes, and I'm left alone in the middle of the flat.

It's not fair, the way he can just run away from a fight.

But I never fought with Jacob before this trip.

The thought leaves me feeling cold, all the way down to the bone.

I wait as long as I can, pacing, pocketing the handful of cash, looping my camera over my shoulder and tugging on my sneakers, doing up the laces slowly, hoping he'll come back. But by ten o'clock, he's still not here.

If I don't leave now, I'm going to be late.

I knock on 1A, expecting Lara, so I'm surprised when Mrs. *Weathershire* opens the door. She's dressed in a house robe, her white hair pulled up in a loose bun.

"Oh, hello!" she says in her chipper way. "You're the Blake girl, aren't you? Is everything all right?"

At first I think I must have the wrong flat, but then Lara appears in the short hall behind her. "She's here to see me, Auntie."

Mrs. Weathershire claps her hands. "Oh, how nice." She leans in close and whispers, "It's about time our Lara made a friend." Then she straightens and steps aside. "Come in, darling. I'll put on the kettle."

"That's all right," says Lara, scooping up her jacket. "We're going for a walk."

We are? I think, but Lara's already pulling me down the stairs. She's wearing leggings and a long-sleeved dress, her hair done in an elaborate fishtail braid. I'm wearing jeans and a sweatshirt, and I can barely manage a neat ponytail.

We're in the front hall when I hear the tread of footsteps overhead.

"Mr. Weathershire?" I venture, glancing up.

Lara rolls her eyes. "Not *everything* is paranormal, Cassidy. Now and then, it's just bad plumbing."

Outside, it's not raining, but it looks like it could, which I'm quickly learning is what the Scots call "partly sunny." A cool breeze cuts through, an instant warning that I'm not dressed warmly enough. But Lara's walking at such a brisk pace down the street, I don't dare ask to go back now.

The road slopes down, away from the Royal Mile. I don't know where we're heading, and Lara isn't exactly chatty, so I search for small talk.

"Are you a fan of Harry Potter?" I ask her.

"Are you asking because I'm English?"

"No," I say, "I'm asking because it's Harry Potter and it's amazing. And the author wrote the books here!"

Lara lifts her chin. "Well, the history of the Elephant

House is contested among locals." She hesitates, adding, "But I've always fancied myself a Ravenclaw."

"So you *are* a fan!"

She cuts a sideways glance at me. "Let me guess, you're a Gryffindor."

I beam. "How did you know?"

She looks me up and down. "Reckless, headstrong, most likely to charge into a situation unprepared." The edge of a smile. "Plus, you're wearing a red and yellow Hogwarts sweatshirt."

I look down at myself. She's right.

At the bottom of the road, she finally slows her pace.

"This is better," she says, breathing deeply. "Not a shred of privacy in that place."

"Mrs. Weathershire is your aunt?"

"My great-aunt, on my mother's side. My father's family is from New Delhi. Mum's family is from Scotland. Hence the . . ." She trails off, gesturing back in the general direction of the Lane's End. "And I was born and raised in London . . . but if I stay here much longer, I'm going to lose my consonants."

I smile, even though I'm not really sure what she means. Lara's accent is crisp, and the Scottish accents I've heard are more musical, but they both sound strange and lovely.

We stop at a kiosk on the street and buy hot chocolate— well, I buy hot chocolate, Lara opts for tea.

She stirs milk into her paper cup, her movements slow, precise. I bet she's the kind of girl with perfect cursive handwriting. The kind who never trips, or bangs her knees, or wakes up with a rat's nest for hair.

"How long are you staying with your aunt?" I ask.

Lara shrugs with a sigh. "My parents didn't exactly give me a return date. They're off on some dig in Tanzania. Something to do with pottery."

"And they didn't take you with them?"

A small, bitter smile. "An archaeological site is apparently no place for a growing girl."

Neither is a ghost tour, I think, suddenly grateful that Mom and Dad didn't decide to leave *me* behind.

"They usually show up again before school starts."

"I'm sorry."

"For what?" she asks curtly.

"I just mean—"

Lara turns on her heel, so fast I almost run into her. "I didn't agree to meet so we could discuss my family life. Let's stick to *business*."

For as long as we've been walking, the castle has loomed overhead on its rocky cliff. Now Lara leads me through a low iron gate and into a kind of park around the cliff's base. We're surrounded by old trees and a few dog-walkers.

Lara sits down primly on a bench in the cliff's shadow. I sit cross-legged, trying not to fidget. She turns her dark-brown eyes on me, one of those long, loaded looks that makes it hard to sit still.

I'm so used to Jacob's constant commentary, like a narrator in my life, that without him, the world feels quiet. He's not always around, but this is the first time it feels like he's deliberately *missing*.

As if Lara can read my mind, too, she says, "No sidekick today?"

"His name is Jacob," I say.

She shrugs dismissively. "Ghosts don't belong in the in-between," she says, "and they certainly don't belong on *this* side of it."

"He saved my life."

"So you let him hitch a ride into the land of the living? Not smart, Cassidy. Not smart at all." She looks around. "And where is he now?"

"Sulking," I say. "He's mad at me for even being here. For talking to you, after what you did."

Lara looks surprised. "What *I* did?"

"To the man in the alley."

"Oh," she says. "The *ghost*." She flicks her fingers dismissively. "Comes with the job. So, how long have you been an in-betweener?"

"A what?"

"An *in-betweener*," she says, drawing out the letters in case I didn't hear. "A betwixter. A shadow-crosser." When I still stare blankly, she rolls her eyes. "You know, what *we* are."

"Oh. I didn't know there was a word for it."

"There are words for everything."

"Like Veil and in-between," I point out.

Lara gives a grudging nod. "Fine, yes. Well, in-between is the one *I* learned, and that makes someone like me—like you—an in-betweener."

"But who taught you?" I ask. "What you are? What to *do*?"

For once, Lara is the one to squirm. "I . . . well . . . that is, no one *taught* me. Uncle Reggie has—*had*—an extensive library. It took a great deal of time and research, a lot of trial and error . . ."

She's lying, I think. Or at least, she's not telling me the whole truth. But before I can call her on it, she changes course.

"You didn't answer *my* question. How long since you *died*?"

I flinch at the word, the blunt way she uses it, but I don't have to do the math. I know exactly how long. I can't seem to forget. "Just over a year," I say, because that's not as weird as saying *three hundred and seventy-three days*.

Lara looks at me, aghast.

"A year?!" she says sharply. "And you haven't reaped a single ghost?"

"I didn't know I was supposed to," I shoot back. I didn't have a user's manual or a library of books (though in truth, there might have been something in Mom and Dad's study, but I never thought to look). "To be honest, I'm still not sure I am."

Lara pinches the bridge of her nose. "Look," she says, "you're drawn to the Veil, aren't you?"

I nod.

"Even though it frightens you . . ."

Yes, I think.

"And part of you wants to forget it's there, but you can't . . ."

Yes.

"You feel compelled to pull back the curtain, step across the line, and find the other side . . ."

"Yes," I confess, barely a whisper.

Lara straightens, nodding triumphantly.

"What you feel, Cassidy Blake, is called a *purpose*."

If Jacob were here, he'd probably make some joke about heroes and quests and monsters waiting to be vanquished. But Jacob's not here, and the only monsters Lara is talking about are ghosts. Like him.

Lara keeps going. "We're drawn to the Veil because it needs us. Because you and I can do something other people can't. We can free the spirits trapped there. We can send them on."

"Do we *have* to?" I ask softly.

Lara purses her lips. "That pull you feel, it doesn't go away. It will just get stronger and stronger until you start holding up your end of the deal."

"But I never made a deal!" I say, exasperated. I didn't choose to go over the bridge that day. I didn't choose to fall into the river. I didn't choose to drown . . . All I wanted was to reach the surface. All I wanted was air and light and a second chance.

A new shadow crosses Lara's face: pity.

"Yes, you did," she says softly. "Maybe you didn't say any special words, but you're sitting here, alive, when you should be dead. Something was given to you, and you have to give it back. You and I—we're able to cross the Veil, we're *meant* to cross it, because we have a job to do on the other side. And it's time you get to work."

CHAPTER SEVENTEEN

urpose.

It's crazy, but I know she's right.

I can feel it in my bones. The answer to the questions I've had for the past year, the ones that have been getting louder and louder since the accident.

Why am I drawn to the Veil?

How am I able to cross it?

What am I supposed to do on the other side?

Lara's hand drifts toward the mirror pendant around her neck.

"How does that work?" I ask, remembering the way she dangled it before the ghost, the incantation pouring from her lips.

Lara draws the necklace over her head and sets it on the bench between us, reflective side up.

"Ghosts can't look at mirrors," she explains. "They get stuck."

I think of Jacob back in the bedroom at the Lane's End, snagged on his own reflection, the terrible version of himself in the glass. And I remember the only answer he would give me.

"I . . . got a little lost . . ."

I wrack my brain—had I ever seen Jacob look into a mirror before that? There wasn't one in my bedroom back home, and he never went into the bathroom—never needed to go. Whenever he passed the thin mirror in the front hall, he always kept walking. I never gave it much thought.

"What do you mean, *stuck*?" I ask.

"Mirrors are honest," says Lara. "They show you as you are. For a ghost, a mirror forces them to face the truth."

"And what's the truth?"

Lara looks at me. She has eyes like stones. Heavy.

"The truth," she says, "is that they're dead. They're gone." She sits back. "In that sense, we're like mirrors, too. *We* show them. *We* tell them. And once you get them to accept the truth, you just reach in and pull out the thread. You should *always* carry something reflective," she adds. "For protection."

"Protection?" I ask. "From what?"

"Not all ghosts are friendly," she says bluntly. "Every time you step into the Veil, you've got one foot in our world, and one foot in theirs. And you may think of yourself as a visitor, a spectator, but the truth is, if a ghost is strong enough, they can hurt you. And they will, because we've got something they *want*."

"What's that?"

Lara taps her chest. "A *life*."

I think of the dull, dark rope she pulled from the ghost's chest. And the strange light that fills my own chest whenever I'm in the Veil. The same light I saw in Lara.

She glances past me. "Oh look," she says dryly. "Your friend is here."

I twist around, and sure enough there's Jacob, scowling at us from behind a nearby tree. Relief rushes through me, and I wish I could throw my arms around him, but the moment he sees me looking, he ducks back out of sight. Only the toe of a sneaker and a chunk of messy blond hair stick out from behind the trunk.

Lara stares down into her cup. "My tea's gone cold." She rises to her feet, sweeping the pendant off the bench. "Back in a tick."

I watch her walk over to the kiosk at the edge of the green. She gets in line, checking her phone as she waits to order.

I catch movement out of the corner of my eye again. This time, Jacob sinks onto the bench beside me. For a few moments, neither one of us speaks. I feel like I should apologize, but also like he should, too, so I'm relieved when I open my mouth to say *sorry* and he cuts me off with, "I shouldn't have disappeared."

"Rule number sixteen of friendship," I say. "Don't go somewhere I can't follow."

"I thought rule number sixteen was never spoil the end of a movie."

"No way," I say confidently, "that's rule number twenty-four."

He chuckles, and it's great to see him smile again, but the space between us still feels tender, like a bruise.

Jacob takes a deep breath. "I didn't tell you," he says slowly, "because I was afraid that if you knew why the ghosts were stuck in the Veil, if you knew that you could send them on, you'd send *me*—"

"But you're not stuck in the Veil."

Jacob looks down. "I *was*."

"Well, you're not anymore. You're here, with me. Do you *want* to leave?"

His head snaps up. "No. Of course not."

"Then why would I send you away? You're my best friend. And I think there's a reason we're all tangled up."

Jacob brightens. "You think?"

I nod emphatically. "You're not an ordinary ghost. I think you're supposed to help me. I think we're supposed to be a team."

He brightens a little. "Like in *Skull and Bone*?"

"Yeah," I say. "Like in *Skull and Bone*."

He cracks a smile. "Which one of us is the dog in this scenario?"

Lara returns, holding a fresh cup of tea. "All right," she says. "Where were we . . . ?"

Jacob leans forward and says, "I still don't like her."

Lara's eyes flick toward him. "I don't like you, either, ghost."

He nearly falls off the back of the bench. "She can hear me?"

"Yes, I can hear you," says Lara, "and I can see you, and I shouldn't be able to do either one of those things, because *you* shouldn't be here."

I clear my throat, eager to change the subject, when I feel it.

The *tap-tap-tap* of a nearby ghost.

Lara feels it, too; I can tell by the way she stiffens, head cocked as if listening for a sound.

"What do you say?" she asks me, turning to go. "Ready to see what you can do?"

CHAPTER EIGHTEEN

L ara doesn't search for the Veil, doesn't grab at air. She simply lifts one hand and slashes it sideways—a single, decisive motion—and the Veil parts around her.

Around us.

I step forward, feel that familiar bloom of cold, and then we're through. We're still in the park at the base of the castle—a bleaker version of it. The world is now gray and ghostly.

I half expected Jacob to stay behind, but he's here, at my side. He lets out a shivery breath and folds his arms. *"Skull and Bone,"* he murmurs, and I don't know if he's talking to me or to himself.

Lara brushes invisible dust from her sleeves, that warm light shining in her chest.

Nearby, a man bundled in winter clothes calls out a

name. His voice is high and thin, as if the wind is stealing it away.

It's beginning to snow, not everywhere, just right around him. When he turns and makes his shuffling way out of the park, the Veil seems to recede with him like a tide, taking the winter with it.

"How . . ." I start.

"The in-between isn't really *one* place," explains Lara. "It's different for every ghost. A kind of . . . time capsule. Ghosts overlap sometimes, bleed together, but in the end, each ghost is living in their own in-between, moving through their own loop."

We follow the man out of the park and down the road. He trudges through shallow snowdrifts up to the door of a house. He shoulders the door open and steps inside. Lara quickens her pace, and we catch up before the door falls shut.

Lara, Jacob, and I step out of the falling snow and into a home. Jacob puts himself in front of me, like a shield. But the man doesn't turn toward us. He stands at a fireplace, stoking the wood of a dying fire with a long iron rod. He's tall and gaunt with wild gray hair and deep-set eyes. He *could* be scary. But he's not. There's just this overwhelming sadness, rippling off him like steam.

"Have you seen him?" asks the man in a low, husky voice.

I take a step forward. "Who?" I ask gently.

Lara is already lifting her pendant, but I catch her wrist, shake my head. "Wait," I whisper.

"Why?" she whispers back. "It isn't necessary to hear his story."

Maybe it's not necessary, but it feels important.

The man's sad eyes drift toward me, to the camera around my neck. "What do you have there, lass?"

I raise it for him to see. "It takes photos."

A shadow crosses the man's face, and I start to think he doesn't know what a photo is. Maybe he lived before cameras existed. But then he draws a small, weathered piece of paper from his shirt and turns it for me to see.

A boy stares out from the yellowed square of an old photograph.

"My son, Matthew," he explains. "Got this taken at the winter fair. Right before he went missing."

My stomach lurches. A child stolen in winter.

The man's eyes go to the window. "My wife, she went south to see her kin. But I couldn't leave my boy. I told his mother I'd wait. I'll wait as long as I have to." The man sinks into his chair by the dying fire and closes his eyes. "I'll wait until he comes home."

Wind whistles against the glass.

The man's breath fogs the air, and I shiver as the cold reaches me.

I'll wait as long as I have to.

I remember what Lara said about ghosts. That they only stay in the Veil because they're stuck. My chest aches for this man trapped here, in this world, in this house, in this endless day of waiting, because I know he'll never stop looking out that window. And I know his son is never coming back.

"Cassidy," says Lara, appearing at my side. I realize that it's time. "Do you have a mirror?" she asks, offering her own.

I nod down to the camera in my hands. "I have this," I say, snapping off the cap and showing her the front lens, the way it shines when I tilt it, reflecting pieces of the room. "Will it work?"

She looks skeptical. "I suppose we'll find out."

I look to Jacob, who's hanging back by the door, his face unreadable.

You're not like him, I think. *You don't belong here. You belong with me.*

Jacob bites his lip, but he nods, and I turn my attention back to the man in the chair. Frost is lacing his beard, and his skin is going white with cold.

"If you see my boy..." he murmurs, his breath a cloud.

"I'll send him home," I promise, lifting the camera. "Can I take your picture, to show him?"

He drags his eyes open, meets his reflection in the lens—and goes still. It's like someone swapped him for a statue instead of a person. He freezes, all the pain and sadness gone from his face.

I hear Jacob suck in a breath, but I keep my focus.

"Do you remember the words?" asks Lara.

I think I do.

"Watch and listen," I say.

Frost crawls over the windowpanes.

"See and know."

Icicles trail down the man's face.

"This is what you are," I whisper.

The man's edges soften, his whole shape rippling. Then I take a deep breath, gather up my nerve, and reach into his chest. I pull out a fragile thread, brittle and gray. Holding the man's life—his death—in my hand, I understand what Lara meant, when she talked about *purpose*. I understand what drew me again and again into the Veil. What I was looking for without looking. What I needed.

It was this.

The ribbon crumbles in my palm, and so does the man—to ash, and then to nothing.

Jacob and Lara and I stand together, silent in the narrow room. Jacob's the first to move. He comes forward and crouches at the foot of the chair, running his fingers through the last of the dust.

And then the room around us begins to thin, like a

photo worn by time, the details wiped away. Of course. The ghost is gone now. It makes sense that his Veil is fading, too.

I feel Lara's hand on my shoulder. "We should go."

Once we're safely on the living side of things again, the three of us walk back to the Lane's End.

Jacob and Lara are a few steps ahead, Jacob peppering her with questions. They seem to be warming to each other. Or at least, reaching a sort of truce.

I hang back. My hand is still prickling strangely from where I held the ribbon of the man's life. His death. It was sad, sending him on, but there was a kind of relief, too, like letting out a breath you've been holding too long. Setting it free.

And afterward, the *tap-tap-tap* was gone.

Not just softer, but vanished, leaving a stretch of quiet, of peace, behind.

It felt . . . *right*.

I quicken my pace to catch up with Jacob and Lara.

"What's the scariest ghost you've ever faced?" Jacob is asking.

Lara taps her finger to her lips. "Couldn't say. It's between William Burke—"

"The—the corpse robber turned serial killer?" stammers Jacob.

"That's the one," says Lara. "It's between him and this little girl in petticoats I found in one of the plague vaults."

Jacob snorts. "A tie between a mass murderer and a girl in a dress?"

Lara shrugs. "Children give me the creeps."

Children. That reminds me.

"Lara," I say, quickening my step even more. "Have you ever seen a woman in a red cloak?"

The humor bleeds from Lara's face, her mouth drawn tight. "Are you talking about the Raven in Red?"

I nod. "Have you ever seen her?"

"Once," she says tightly. "Last winter. I was visiting for the holidays, hunting in the in-between, when I heard her singing. And the next thing I knew, I was walking straight toward her outstretched hand." Lara shakes her head. "It was a near thing."

"But you got away."

"I got *lucky*. Aunt Alice was nearby, I heard her calling, and it broke the spell. I had just enough sense to twist free and leave the in-between. And I've been very, very careful ever since." Lara's dark eyes narrow. "Why? Have *you* seen her, Cassidy?"

I nod, and Lara's hand shoots out, stopping me in my tracks. "You have to stay away from her, do you understand?" There's an urgency in her voice. It's wrong on her, out of place. "Remember what I said about our lives?" Her hand goes to her chest, to the place where the light shone through in the Veil. "About the ghosts who want them? The Raven is one of those. She feeds on the threads of the children she steals. But those threads are small and thin. She has to eat a lot of them just to be what she is. But if she got ahold of a life like yours, or mine—something bright—it would be *disastrous*."

I shudder at the thought.

Lara looks to Jacob. "Do your job, ghost. Keep her safe."

Jacob snorts. "Easier said than done."

We climb the hill that leads back to the Lane's End.

"It doesn't make sense," Lara says, half to herself. "It isn't the right time of year."

"I know." It's been bothering me, too. What was it Findley said? *She comes with the cold.* I think of the river, my fall into the icy stream. The way the cold reaches for me every time I cross the Veil. The bluish edge to the light in my chest.

"Maybe it has something to do with the way I . . ." It's still hard to say out loud, even now, even with someone like Lara. I change course. "What does the Veil feel like, when you step through it?" I ask her.

Lara thinks. "Like a fog. A fever. I was ill once, really ill. It was touch and go for a bit," she adds briskly. "And I couldn't stay awake. It feels like that. Dreamy, but not in a good way."

I nod. "For me, it feels like falling into a frozen river. It feels like bitter cold. If the Raven is drawn to cold, then maybe she's drawn to me."

"Maybe," says Lara. "Well, that's even *more* reason to stay away from her. If you do see her, cover your ears, get out of the Veil, and for goodness' sake," she adds, nodding at my camera, "get yourself a proper mirror."

We're nearly back to the Lane's End, when I recognize the man ambling toward us, his crown of red hair catching the sun. I slam to a stop at the sight.

"Uh-oh," says Jacob.

"What have we here?" says Findley. He looks at Lara. "Miss Chowdhury. I never took *you* for a rule breaker."

Lara straightens. "I haven't broken any rules," she says, once again the picture of primness. The wind has blown my brown curls all over the place. How is it her black braid is still perfectly in order?

"What are you doing here?" I squeak at Findley.

"Funny thing, that," he says. "Your parents sent me to check on *you*. Only you weren't there."

I glance at Lara. "I might have promised my parents I would stay inside," I tell her. I swivel back to Findley. "We were just getting some fresh air."

"Is that so?" he says, a glimmer in his eye. I know that spark. I've seen it on Mom's face a hundred times.

"I'm not in trouble, am I?"

"Och," he says amiably, "a little wandering never hurt anyone."

Which I'm pretty sure isn't true, especially when it comes to young people and foreign cities full of child-snatching ghosts, but I appreciate the sentiment.

"Tell you what." He holds up a meaty finger. "I won't tell your folks on one condition."

"What's that?"

"Well," he says, "your mom and dad sent me to see if you were feeling brave enough to join them up at the castle."

"I wasn't scared," I snap.

"No shame in being scared," he counters. "But there's a difference between being scared and being scared *away*. Come with, and I'll look like a right champion for changing your mind. You're welcome to come, too, Miss Chowdhury."

I glance at Lara, who shrugs. "I'll pass," she says. "The castle *is* a fascinating site," she adds with a weighted look. It flicks from me to Jacob and back. "Just remember what I told you."

"Or," says Jacob, "we could just go back up to the nice, warm place with comic books and tea cakes."

"Look now," says Findley, seeing me hesitate. "You can't come to Edinburgh and *not* see the castle."

"We can see it from here," says Jacob, pointing at the building on the cliff.

"Aren't you just a wee bit curious?" continues Findley.

Of course I'm curious. I've never been inside a castle. Plus, my head's full of Lara's talk about purpose, and my hands are still warm from sending on the man in the house.

"Well?" prompts Findley. "What do you say?"

I look at Jacob.

I want to see the castle, but I don't want to go without him, and not just because I might get stuck in the Veil. It was weird, him not being there this morning. I felt like someone had cut my shadow away.

But Jacob's not just my shadow.

He's my partner in crime.

The sidekick to my hero (*or hero to my sidekick*, I amend when he looks at me aghast). And he should have a say.

It's up to you, I think. *If you don't want to go, we don't have to go.*

And maybe he just wanted to be given the choice, because he rolls his eyes and flashes me a grin. "Well," he says, "I've read all the comics, and I can't eat the cakes."

I smile and turn to Findley.

"All right. Let's go to the castle."

CHAPTER NINETEEN

Edinburgh Castle sits on its high rock cliff, looming over *everything*. As we start up the broad stone steps, it stares back at us, a dark gray shadow against a pale gray sky.

As we climb, Findley rambles about the castle's many famous ghosts. His eyes grow brighter with every story. There's the piper who went missing in the tunnels, and the soldiers lost during a siege, and a headless drummer, and the prisoners left in the vaults, and a woman accused of witchcraft and burned at the stake. The Veil is growing heavier with every story and with each upward step. The weight of history, of memories. Of things no longer *here*, but not *gone*, either.

Findley leads us over an empty moat and through the front gate onto the castle grounds.

The word *castle* has always made me think of a giant house.

But this is more like a miniature city.

We're still outdoors, surrounded by high stone walls and a network of lower buildings, some steepled and others flat, all of it like something out of a medieval fantasy.

"*Cool,*" whispers Jacob.

The Veil's gray curtain flutters at the edges of my sight. If I crossed over here, what would I see? Curiosity blooms inside my chest. But I know now that it's not just curiosity. It's the pull of purpose. My heart picks up. My fingers curl around the camera.

I don't realize I've stopped walking until Findley glances back.

"This way!" he shouts. He leads us through what he calls a "portcullis"—it's a gate like the top half of a mouth, full of sharp steel teeth.

We go up, and up, and up, all the way to the top, to a courtyard ringed with cannons and studded with tourists. The producers clearly couldn't shut down a place this popular to film my parents.

"I don't see them," says Jacob, but Findley is already beelining for the edge of the battlements. I don't know what he's looking at, not until I get close enough to see the view beyond the stone wall.

View doesn't do it justice. We're so high up, with the castle buildings at our backs and the steep drop-off of the cliff. All of Edinburgh rolls away like a carpet beneath us.

"Wow," says Jacob.

"Wow," I echo.

"See?" says Findley, beaming. "I told you it was worth the trip."

He's right.

This place is *breathtaking*. For once, I can't bring myself to take a picture, because I know a photo could never really capture what I'm seeing. So I lean on the ramparts and simply take it all in. The Veil shudders and ripples, and I close my eyes, imagining I can hear the distant thud of soldiers' boots, the thunder of cannons, the mournful song of a bagpipe, and . . .

Singing.

I shiver.

Do you hear that? I ask Jacob silently, but when he answers, he sounds distracted.

"It's probably the wind."

But it's not the wind. Way up here, the air whistles around us, but there's more than air to that sound I heard.

That voice.

I know it by the way the music echoes in my bones. I try to remember Lara's words, her warnings, but my own thoughts keep unraveling, and I have to hold on tight just to keep them from floating away.

"Cass?" Jacob waves a translucent hand in front of my face.

I blink, and the singing fades, replaced by only the high, thin breeze. Maybe Jacob was right. Maybe it was just a trick of the air.

I step away from the rampart, just as something goes *BOOM*.

I jump, lurching back, but it's clear I'm not the only one who heard *that*. A plume of smoke goes up nearby, and the air shakes with the sound. Findley only smiles.

"One o'clock cannon," he says, as if it's perfectly normal for people to fire heavy artillery in the middle of the day. "Come on," he adds. "We'd best go find your parents."

I pull the show's filming schedule from my pocket, but all it says is *CASTLE*. Not incredibly helpful, considering this castle takes up a whole mountaintop.

"Do you have any idea where they are?" I ask Findley.

"No," he admits. "But it shouldn't be that hard to find them. I'm guessing the barracks or the prison cells."

Right. Makes sense. My parents aren't here for the crown jewels, or the kitchens, or St. Margaret's Chapel— each site proudly advertised by a placard or sign. No, they'll be knee-deep in the darker part of the castle's history.

We cut through the nearest building, which, according to the banner on the wall, is the Great Hall. My first thought is that it looks like the dining hall straight out of Harry Potter.

"Pigworts!" announces Jacob triumphantly. "Broom ball! Crowpuff!"

He's never actually read the books, which he knows drives me crazy, but he also knows I don't have time to sit and turn ten thousand pages for him, so I broke down and showed him the movies.

"It's like that scene with Tumbledore and the Magic Hat!" he exclaims gleefully.

He clearly wasn't paying that much attention.

We make our way from the Great Hall out into another, smaller courtyard. Here, the spell is broken by signs for public restrooms, and a little touristy café.

"Kind of kills the mood, doesn't it?" says Jacob.

Findley stops to grab a paper cup of strong black tea. I look around, trying to figure out why the castle feels so different from Mary King's Close. Maybe it's the number of tourists, or the open air . . . According to Findley, this place is definitely haunted. And I can feel the Veil, but it doesn't feel menacing. There's a low and steady *tap-tap-tap* of ghosts, but it's like a light drizzle, not a downpour.

Is it just me, I think, *or is this place way less scary than Mary King's Close?*

"Shhh!" hisses Jacob. "Don't say that!"

Why not?

"You'll jinx us."

I roll my eyes.

And then we step out of the courtyard and down into the prisons, and all that nice not-so-haunted feeling goes away, sucked out like heat through an open window.

I shiver, the air around me suddenly cold. The ceilings are low, the walls broken by iron bars, messages scrawled on the backs of cells like fingernails dug into wood. All the hairs on my arm stand up in warning.

Jacob scowls at me. "You did this."

"I didn't jinx us," I whisper out loud. "The castle was already haunted."

"Maybe." He glowers. "But you definitely made it *more* haunted."

I want to tell him that's not how it works, but the Veil is already wrapping itself around me, trying to drag me down, under. The *tap-tap-tap* turns to hammering. I retreat a few steps toward the safety of the courtyard. Then I hear Dad's voice, the one he uses when he's teaching a class.

"We've moved from a buried town to a looming fortress. The Edinburgh Castle sits on a shelf of jagged stone, standing guard for nearly fourteen hundred years . . ."

"With that much history," chimes in Mom, "it's no wonder the castle is home to so many ghosts . . ."

Of course their voices aren't coming from the airy, ghost-free courtyard at our backs, but from down the hall, deeper within the prison.

As if Findley can tell I'm about to bolt, he plants a large hand on my back and urges me forward into the dark. We find my parents standing in a cell, the light from the camera crew casting jagged shadows through the bars.

"Prisoners of war were kept in these very cells," says Mom, "and if you look closely, you can see their scrawled and desperate messages. Of course, these aren't the only things they left behind."

I hear a dull knocking, like a fist against iron bars.

No one else seems to notice.

I grip my camera.

"And cut!" calls one of the crew.

Mom sees Findley and then me, and her face breaks into a smile.

"Cassidy!"

"There's our girl," says Dad. "Well done, Findley, coaxing her out."

"Wasn't hard," he says, shooting me a conspiratorial look. "I think she was getting restless."

"You missed the South Bridge Vaults," says Mom, wrapping an arm around my shoulders. I try to look disappointed, even though I'm just relieved.

And I'm even more relieved when they wrap filming and we get out of the prisons. We head back into the open air of the courtyard. The crew heads for their next location, the castle barracks, but my steps slow. Not because I'm scared, but because there's music on the air again, high and sweet and haunting.

"That's because there's a bagpiper," says Jacob. And he's right. It's just a man in a kilt standing on the battlements above, the instrument wailing softly in his hands.

There's nothing strange about the bagpiper—so why do I have such a strange feeling? Maybe I'm just borrowing trouble, as Mom would say. Looking for monsters in the closet. Shapes in the dark. I'm probably still on edge after what happened with the man in the house. Shaken up by the whole sending-ghosts-on.

It was pretty intense.

Dad glances back from where he stands at a set of doors. "Cass? You coming?"

"I'll be right behind you," I say, nodding at a restroom sign. Jacob waits outside while I duck in. I snap the cap back on my camera lens and set it on the counter, splashing a little water on my face. My nerves settle, and I sigh, take up the camera again, and head back outside.

But Jacob's not there.

Jacob? I call for him, inside my head, and then out loud. "Jacob?"

No answer.

It's like he just *disappeared*. Only, he wouldn't do that again, not after this morning.

"Jacob?" I call again, louder.

And then there's a lull in the bagpiper's song.

Jacob's voice reaches me, but it's thin, wispy. *"Cassidy . . ."*

I turn, scanning the courtyard. *Where are you?*

Why can't I see him? Why does his voice sound so far away?

And then it hits me. The Veil.

But why would he cross over without me?

I'm coming! I think, reaching for the gray curtain.

"Stay ba—" he starts, but his voice cuts off suddenly, and I'm already tearing the fabric aside, tumbling out of one world and into another.

Cold water and numb skin and all the air knocked out of me, and then I'm through.

It takes my eyes a split second to adjust.

To the grayed-out world and the light inside my chest.

To the tourists suddenly replaced by soldier ghosts marching in the castle square.

To the sight of Jacob's panicked face, visible for only an instant before he's dragged backward into the prisons.

I don't think then.

It never occurs to me to run away, to run *any* other direction except toward my best friend.

"Jacob!" I shout, racing after him.

Afterward, I will regret so much about this moment. The fact that I didn't have a plan. The fact that I didn't take the cap off my camera. The fact that I simply ran.

But in this moment, all I can think of is saving Jacob.

I plunge into the darkened prison.

The cells aren't empty anymore.

Men in ragged uniforms rattle the bars, but I'm not paying attention to any of them because Jacob's there, on the ground of a far cell, being pinned to the damp stone floor by a half dozen children.

Two of them look like they belong in a fancy old painting, and one is dressed in rags. Others look more modern, like they could even go to my school. The only thing they have in common is the cold pallor of their skin, and the fact that they're all attacking my friend.

Hands clamp over Jacob's mouth and knees pin his wrists. One frost-covered boy sits on his chest as the other kids fight to hold him down.

"Get off him!" I order, hurrying toward the cell.

Jacob tears his mouth free long enough to shout, "Run!" but I can't, I won't, not without him.

"Get away from my friend," I snarl, lifting the camera. But the cap is still on, and before I can get it off, a hand catches my wrist, and a voice whispers in my ear.

"Sorry, love," it says. "They only listen to me."

The hand tightens, and I'm wrenched around. For an instant, all I see is the red of her cloak. Then, glossy black curls, white skin, crimson lips that curl into a sweet smile.

"Hello, dearest," coos the Raven in Red. I know I need to fight, but I can't, not with her fingers on my skin and her eyes on my eyes and her voice like music in my head.

"You . . ." I murmur, but I can't even hold on to my thoughts.

Her other hand drifts up to my chin, tilting my face toward hers. "So much light, so much warmth."

"Cassidy!" screams Jacob, and I snap back to my senses, but it's too late.

The Raven in Red changes before me.

Her cloak whips violently, as if caught in a gust of wind, and her fingers harden like claws. Her smile cracks and turns cruel, and she thrusts her hand straight into my chest.

Cold rushes through me, a bone-chilling cold, worse than the bottom of the river. It feels like icy fingers wrapped around my heart.

I can't breathe, can't speak, can't do anything but watch as the Raven draws out her hand, clutching a ribbon of blue-white light. My light. My life.

She tears it free.

And everything goes dark.

PART FOUR

THE RAVEN IN RED

CHAPTER TWENTY

Cass . . . Cassidy! Oh god, Cassidy, wake up!"

I open my eyes and see gray.

It takes me a second to remember where I am, another to realize I'm lying on my back. I stare up at the dim, slick stones of the prison ceiling.

Jacob crouches next to me, nails digging into my shoulder, and I know something's wrong because I don't just feel his grip—it hurts. His hand is solid on my arm. Like flesh and bone.

"What happened?" I ask. It comes out a groggy mumble.

Jacob helps me sit up. I look down at myself and gasp. I'm washed out, faded like a picture, like Jacob, like every other ghost in the Veil. But it's not the lack of color that startles me. It's the lack of light. The glow behind my ribs, that steady blue-white coil, is *gone*.

It all comes rushing back then.

The Raven in Red.

Her hand reaching through my chest.

The bright ribbon wrapped around her fingers.

Another memory collides with it—Lara putting her hand to her own chest.

We've got something they want.

If she got ahold of a life like yours . . . it would be disastrous.

I stagger to my feet, head spinning.

"Where is she?"

The cells to every side are filled with prisoner ghosts, but I barely register any of them as I stumble up the stairs and out into the castle courtyard.

The square is full of ghost soldiers carrying bayonets, men in fine-cut clothes, women in corseted dresses. But there's no sign of the Raven.

I reach out to grab the Veil, to wrench it aside and plunge back into the world of the living. But my fingers close on nothing but air.

No.

Not again.

"Cassidy," says Jacob, but I have to focus.

I close my eyes and try to imagine the gray cloth against my fingers, the curtain brushing my palms, and—

I catch hold of something, something thin, but there.

I open my eyes, let out a shaky breath when I see the Veil in my hands. But when I try to pull the fabric aside, I can't.

I can't find the part in the curtain.

Because there *is* no part. The Veil warps around my fingers, bending slightly with the pressure, but no matter how I pull, the curtain doesn't let me through. I throw my weight against the gray cloth, and it stretches, pulls tight, but doesn't break.

No wonder it's so hard for ghosts to touch our world, to leave any kind of mark.

But I'm not a ghost.

I'm an in-betweener. A betwixter. A *Veil* crosser.

That means I've got a foot on either side.

That means I can get back.

I have to be able to get back.

Jacob's saying something, but I can't hear him, not over the white noise of panic in my ears.

And the shock when I see *her*.

She's all the way across the courtyard, and on the other side of the Veil. But I *can* see her, clear as glass, as if someone cut a window through the fog. Her red cloak. Her black hair. The light of my life coiled around her hand.

The Raven looks back at me, across the Veil, and smiles.

And then she turns and slips through the crowd.

I can't let her get away with this.

I can't let her get *away*.

But she's already gone, and I'm left banging on the Veil as it hardens from curtain to wall against my hands.

Jacob's voice finally registers.

"I'm so sorry, Cass. I tried to warn you it was a trap. You shouldn't have come after me."

"I had to," I say, but the words sound thin, even to me. I look down at my hands again. They're not as bright as they should be. Not as colorful. Not as real.

No. No. No. The word rattles in my head. I don't know if it's denial or the fact that I'm trapped in the Veil like all the other ghosts, and just like them, I can't face the truth. The truth, that without that light, without that life, I'm . . . the opposite of living, I'm . . . I'm dea—

"*No,*" says Jacob with sudden energy. "You are *not* the opposite of living. You are just *temporarily without a life*. And those are very different things. You see, one is gone forever and the other is simply *misplaced*, so all we have to do is *find* your life and get it back."

I'm usually the one dragging Jacob away from morbid thoughts. And even if he's trying too hard to make me believe, I'm still relieved he's trying. It gives me something to hold on to.

"Cassidy . . . ?"

I turn at the sound of my name. It's coming from far away, distorted by the Veil, drawn out into something high and thin. But I know that voice. I have always known that voice. *Mom.*

And suddenly, my panic turns a different shade.

"Mom!" I call back, but my voice comes out like the opposite of an echo, muted. She'll never hear me.

I press myself against the Veil, straining to see out of the world of the dead and into the land of the living. It's like shoving your face into a bowl of water, no air, and everything's kind of swimmy.

"Cassidy . . . ?"

It's Dad calling this time. At first, his tone is casual, as if they simply haven't spotted me. As if I've wandered off again. Just like before. But every time my parents say my name, their voices get tighter, higher, the worry creeping in.

"I'm right here!" I shout, and all around the courtyard, the old-fashioned men and women turn their heads.

But beyond the Veil, my parents keep calling my name.

I can see them, but they can't see me.

I can hear them, but they can't hear me.

And suddenly I believe what Lara said, about ghosts not being in the Veil by choice. About them being trapped.

Ghosts don't stay because they want to.

They stay because they can't move on.

Dad pulls his cell phone from his coat and my heart picks up as I dig for the emergency phone in my pocket. I clutch it until my fingers ache. But I already know it won't work.

Dad dials, waits, but the phone in my hand never rings.

Findley appears beside my parents, his Scottish lilt little more than a whisper through the thickening wall. ". . . I'm sure she hasn't gone far . . ."

He has no idea how right he is.

"We'll find her . . ." he continues.

I turn toward Jacob, desperate. "You have to get their attention. You have to *do* something out there."

Jacob pales. "Cass, I've never been able to—"

"Please," I beg. "You have to try."

Jacob swallows, then gives a determined nod. "Okay," he says. "Stay here."

As if I have a choice.

He reaches out, and the Veil manifests around his fingers, solid but pliant, bending. For a second, as he presses against the curtain and the fog thins, I can see the world beyond, and I think it's going to work.

But then Jacob's hand begins to shake, and the Veil repels him. Jacob stumbles backward, and my heart sinks.

"I don't understand," he says, rubbing his fingers.

But I think I do.

Jacob and I have always been tangled up, tied together.

And he's always been able to cross over, but that was when *I* could, too. He could come into my world, and I could go into his. But now that I'm trapped here, so is he.

A soldier ghost cuts in front of us, blocking my view. The Veil ripples, and the world beyond it fades like a dream.

"S'no place for children," growls the soldier, gesturing at the castle yard. "Get ye gone, or I'll toss you in a prison cell."

My parents' voices are fading.

"Wait," I say, trying to slip past the soldier. He cuffs me around the collar and shoves me backward into Jacob. We go stumbling onto the cobblestones, the soldier glowering at us. Jacob gets up and pulls me to my feet.

"Come on," he says in my ear. "We can't stay here."

But I can't just leave my parents, either.

Jacob wraps his arms around me and squeezes. "We're going to figure this out."

His voice is an anchor. His words are a raft.

"You're right," I say.

I have to get my life back.

I pull free and start toward the castle gate, forcing myself away from my parents and Findley and the crew, away from the sound of my name on the air. Jacob doesn't have to ask where we're going. He can read my mind, so he already knows.

We're going to get help.

CHAPTER TWENTY-ONE

S ometimes help is a place and sometimes it's a person, and sometimes it's a bit of both.

We set out on foot, racing off the castle grounds, through the portcullis and the front gate.

We have to get to the Lane's End.

We have to find Lara.

We hurry down the broad set of steps, and it spits us out at the top of the Royal Mile. The other Edinburgh is gone, swept behind the curtain. Here in the Veil, a stranger, older city takes shape, brimming with—well, not life, but movement. People.

This is the *real* city of ghosts.

They're everywhere, some in modern dress and others in old-fashioned clothes. As I watch a dozen different scenes play out, it's clear enough that Lara was right—every ghost is trapped inside their own time, their own loop.

Mourners gather under a sea of umbrellas.

A woman in a long dress pushes an ornate stroller, cooing to its hidden contents.

A cluster of men wearing kilts stumbles past, their accents too thick to understand.

"Get back here!" bellows a man, and I turn, thinking he's talking to me, but a second later, a small boy darts past us clutching a loaf of bread. The vendor charges after as the boy races into the street, right out in front of a horse and carriage.

I reach to catch his arm, but I'm too late. The boy trips, and the horse rears up, and I squeeze my eyes shut, waiting for the crash, the screams, but they don't come. A moment later, the boy and the man and the horse and carriage are gone. Somewhere the loop begins again.

"Come on, Cass," says Jacob, taking my hand.

We turn off the Royal Mile and the world flickers, shifts. It's like moving from room to room in an endless house. There are moments when it seems empty, a blank gray canvas, and others when the ghosts and memories layer so thick it's hard to focus.

A woman in vintage clothes storms out of a doorway.

Threads of smoke billow up from a building down the street.

A man in a hooded cloak warns people to stay inside.

I've never been in the Veil this long. Things should be getting murky by now, but instead, they're getting clearer. I don't feel dizzy, or foggy, or lost, or any of the other things that a *living* person is supposed to feel if they spend too long in the land of the dead.

This is a bad sign, and I know it, and so does Jacob, who clutches my hand as we race toward the Lane's End. But the closer we get, the more I feel like I'm going the wrong way. Which doesn't make any sense.

Turn around, say my legs.

Go this way, say my arms.

Follow me, says my heart.

But I can't trust any of them, not here in the Veil.

The Lane's End comes into sight, and a small sob of relief escapes my throat. I'm so glad to see that bright red door.

I try not to dwell on what it means, that the Lane's End exists here inside the Veil. That someone's last moments must be rooted in this place.

I throw open the door.

"Lara!" I call into the front hall.

"Lara!" shouts Jacob as we climb the stairs to 1A.

She probably can't hear us, not across the Veil, but we call out anyway.

The door to her flat hangs open and we step inside. It looks older, stranger, piled with books and wallpapered differently. Of course, this isn't *Lara's* flat. But right now, it's as close as I can get.

I have to hope it's close enough.

I press myself against the Veil, trying to see through a curtain that seems to be getting thicker with every passing second. When the world beyond finally comes into view, it's out of focus, like staring at two strips of film that haven't been lined up quite right.

My heart sinks, because blurry or not, I can see that the flat is empty.

I should be surprised, but I'm not. I knew she wouldn't be here. I just don't know *how* I knew.

"Hullo, hullo," says a low voice behind me.

Jacob jumps, and I spin around to find an older man in a robe. He has a pipe between his lips and a book under one arm. He's a ghost, that part's obvious, but there's something about him that also seems . . . solid. Present. With the grieving father in the freezing house, it was clear we'd stepped into his memory. Even when he talked to me, he was in a deep fog.

But this man doesn't seem to be stuck in a loop. When he looks at me, at Jacob, I can tell he really sees us.

"Can I help you?" he asks in a kind voice.

"I'm . . . looking for Lara," I stammer.

"Ah, I'm afraid my niece isn't home."

"Your niece?"

"How rude," says the man, holding out his hand. "I'm Reginald Weathershire. My friends call me Reggie."

Of course. *Mr.* Weathershire.

The Lane's End—this must be *his* Veil.

"Cassidy Blake," I say, shaking his hand.

Mr. Weathershire frowns. "She mentioned you. But"—he shakes his head—"she said you were"—he gestures to my shirtfront, where the light should be—"like her."

"I'm not a ghost," I say, cringing at the word. "It's just been a very long day."

"Hi, I'm Jacob," Jacob cuts in, "and not to be rude, but we're kind of in a hurry. Do you know where your niece went?"

Mr. Weathershire shakes his head. "Afraid I don't get out much these days."

Panic fills my lungs like water.

How am I supposed to find Lara?

I turn in a slow circle, trying to figure out what to do. But the Veil doesn't have any answers. I close my eyes and force myself to breathe, focus on the air going into my lungs, the tug inside my chest—

Wait.

A tug?

It's there, right behind my ribs, the same pull I felt when I first met Lara. Like there was a thread running between us. I feel it now, only it's not pulling me into the flat but out into the hall, down the stairs.

"We have to go."

"Wait, where?" asks Jacob.

"I think I know how to find her," I say, already heading for the door.

But something makes me look back.

Mr. Weathershire is across the room, sliding his book into a gap on his shelf. According to Lara, he's a ghost, and he should be sent on. But he doesn't look lost. He doesn't seem trapped.

"Why are you here?" I ask.

He looks around fondly. "Suppose I'm not ready to say goodbye."

"And Lara lets you stay?"

He chuckles softly. "We all need someone who sees us clearly."

Huh. Maybe Lara has a soft spot after all.

"And maybe I'm Skull Shooter," says Jacob. "No offense, Cass, but I don't care about Lara's inner Hufflepuff. I care about getting your life back, and to do that, we need to *find* her."

Jacob's right, of course.

I follow the pull, let it lead me down the stairs and out onto the street. Mom always says to trust your gut, so I do.

Have you ever stood at the top of a hill? There's that natural urge to go down, the way your legs pick up momentum once you start, the pull of gravity sending you always, always, always toward the base of the slope.

That's what it feels like now.

Like Lara is the bottom of the hill, and I'm being drawn toward her.

All I have to do is trust my feet, and walk.

CHAPTER TWENTY-TWO

I know it sounds crazy," I say, explaining the pull I feel as we make our way through the ghostly city.

Jacob shrugs. "It's not the weirdest thing that's happened today."

I laugh—a small, frantic sound. He knocks my shoulder.

The Veil ebbs and flows around us, buildings going up and coming down, ghosts flickering past. I should have listened to my limbs when they told me I was going the wrong way. Now I let them lead me. I don't ignore the tug, the voice in my bones that says go this way or that. My feet carry me, and with every step, the line between me and Lara tightens and tightens and tightens until . . . it starts to go slack.

I slam to a stop.

Thinking I've gone the wrong way, I backtrack several

feet until the tension returns. I try again, but no matter where I go from here, the line slackens.

This—right here—is where I'm supposed to be.

The problem is, *right here* isn't anywhere.

The Veil is empty, except for smudges of street and the smoky outlines of places that don't exist on this side of the curtain. It's like one of those paintings where the artist leaves the sketch lines at the edges. This is an edge, a spot where the Veil and the regular world don't line up.

I squint, trying to make out the other side, but it's getting harder to see anything beyond the curtain. When I try, everything's out of focus, and—

Focus.

That gives me an idea.

My camera is still hanging around my neck. It may be a weird camera, one that sees a little less and a little more. But *all* cameras allow you to adjust for different focal lengths, so you can focus on things that are up close or things that are far away. Like the Veil, and the regular world.

I lift the cracked viewfinder to my eye, turning the lens until the Veil in front of me blurs. For a second, the whole picture is out of focus, but I keep turning the lens until the Veil becomes a haze, and the real world beyond comes into sharp relief.

If we were in the real world right now, we'd be standing inside a bookstore.

BLACKWELL'S, reads a sign on the wall in white and blue paint.

"Follow me," I tell Jacob.

He keeps a hand on my shoulder, and I keep my eye to the viewfinder as we weave through a maze of customers and bookshelves.

Down, says the tug in my chest, and I take the stairs, moving through a world I can see but not touch, passing through people as if they're not even there—when really, I'm the one who's missing.

We reach the bottom floor, and there she is, in a corner of the bookstore café. She's sitting at a small round table, stirring a cup of tea and reading a book.

"Lara!" I shout, hoping her senses are more tuned than mine.

She glances up, and my hopes soar for a second before she looks back at her book.

"Lara, please."

A slight crease forms between her eyes, but that's it.

I reach out and push her as hard as I can. Or at least, I try. My hand hits the Veil, and it feels more like glass than fabric. The glass trembles, but doesn't bend or break.

Lara gets to her feet, shuts the book, and starts to leave.

No.

I follow her out of the café, Jacob on my heels.

"Lara Lara Lara Lara Lara—" he calls as she rounds the corner into an empty aisle, promptly spins on one heel, and steps smoothly through the Veil.

"*What?*" she hisses.

I let my camera fall back on its strap. The bookstore shimmers like the afterimage of a flash, bright and gone, bright and gone.

But Lara is there.

Real.

"So you *did* hear us," says Jacob.

"Yes, I heard you, ghost," she snaps.

"My name," he shoots back, "is *Jacob*."

I don't have time for any of this.

"Lara," I say. "We have a problem."

Her attention finally shifts my way, a smart reply already forming on her lips. But at the sight of me, gray and faded and lightless, she stops. For the first time since we met, Lara looks truly surprised. I didn't think it was possible to faze her, and I'm not sure if it makes me proud or terrified.

"Cassidy . . ." she murmurs.

I thought my current state might merit some concern, but I'm still caught off guard when the next words out of her mouth are, "What have you *done*?"

"I didn't *do* anything!" I counter.

"I warned you," says Lara, hands on her hips. "I told you to stay away from the Raven. And you—" She turns on Jacob. "I told you to protect her." Back to me. "I left you alone for an hour and you go and lose your thread?!"

"You're really not helping," I say, fighting to keep the panic from my voice.

"What were you thinking?" she continues. "Where was your camera?"

I duck my head. "The cap was on."

Lara throws up both hands. "That's just great, Cassidy." She sighs, pinching the bridge of her nose. "How did you even find me?"

"I don't know," I say. "I just kind of *knew*. Like there was a rope, running between us."

Lara nods. Her eyes narrow in what I'm coming to recognize is her thinking face. "It makes sense, that we'd be drawn together. After all, like calls to like. I've felt it, too, but I didn't realize it had a *use* . . ."

"Not to interrupt your brainstorming," says Jacob, "but Cass is CURRENTLY A GHOST."

It's the first time I've heard the words out loud. It turns my stomach.

"Don't be dramatic," Lara says. "You're just stuck in the Veil," she tells me. "Your life thread has been stolen. We need to steal it *back*. Tell me exactly what happened."

So I do.

I tell her about the castle, the creepy children, the Raven in Red, and the way she stole my life. Lara listens to the whole story in silence, arms crossed and eyes cast upward. She stays that way, even after I've finished.

"Say something," I plead as an uncomfortable silence settles over us.

"I'm thinking."

"Think faster," says Jacob.

All of a sudden, a shiver rolls through me, and for an instant, my lungs ache and the world dims, and I feel so cold, I can't imagine ever being warm again.

"Cass?" says Jacob, his eyes wide with worry. "What was that?"

"I don't know," I whisper, trying to keep the tremble from my voice. But when I look down at my hands, they seem . . . grayer.

"You really don't look good," says Lara, which is a totally unhelpful comment. Her own warm light shines brightly through her shirt.

"I want my life back," I say through chattering teeth.

Lara bites her lip. "All right, do you want the good news, or the bad?"

"I could really use some good news right now."

"The good news is, the Raven doesn't *own* your life yet. It's still yours. She's just borrowing it."

"And the bad news?" I ask.

Lara hesitates. "The bad news is what she's going to do with it."

I don't even want to ask. But I don't have a choice.

"What?"

"Well," says Lara. "She has to dig up her own body and put your life inside it. I guess that's another piece of good news—it does take time to dig up a body, so we have until she manages that. But I guess that's also the bad news. Once she places your life thread inside her body, well, there's no untying that knot." Lara looks down at her watch. "There are five historical graveyards in Edinburgh, and it's safe to assume she'll go to one of them . . ."

I'm so caught up in the good news/bad news seesaw that it takes me a moment to remember—I know that answer. Findley already told me.

"She's buried in Greyfriars."

Lara brightens. "Well, *that's* a step in the right direction. Greyfriars is not far from here. Let's go."

Lara turns, but I catch her arm. "Wait. You can't come with us."

"You need me there."

And she's right. "I know. But I need you to do something else first."

"What could possibly be more important—"

"You have to find my parents."

Lara blanches. "What?"

"They're up at the castle—or at least they were—look for the filming crew and Findley, and—"

"And what exactly am I supposed to tell them?" snaps Lara. "That their daughter got snatched up by some creepy Scottish legend?"

I pause for a second, wondering if Mom and Dad would actually believe that. But their interest in the supernatural only goes so far.

"Just tell them I'm *okay*—"

"I'm not big on lying—"

"Make an exception. *Please*."

Lara shakes her head but says, "Fine."

I throw my arms around her. Lara goes stiff, then gives my back a small pat. I try not to think about how different she feels compared to me, how much more solid and *real*.

"I'll tell them *something*," she says, pulling away, "and then I'll meet you at Greyfriars." She turns to go, one hand lifted to the Veil. But before she parts the curtain, she looks back.

"Cassidy."

"Yes?"

"We're going to fix this," she says.

And then the curtain ripples, and she's gone.

CHAPTER
TWENTY-THREE

There's no sun in the Veil, only a wan gray glow, but the sky somehow darkens around us as Jacob and I head for Greyfriars Kirk. As if someone's cast a shadow over everything.

Fog slips through the streets, and the presence of ghosts feels suddenly menacing.

I grip the camera in both hands, cap off and lens ready, in case of trouble.

"I don't suppose we have a *plan*," says Jacob.

"Sure," I say, trying to sound hopeful. "The plan is to stop the Raven in Red and get my life back."

"I hate to point this out, but neither one of us has a *physical form*."

"I know."

"And the Raven is on the other side of the Veil."

"I know."

"And we can't—"

"I *know*," I snap. Jacob cringes.

I take a deep breath. "Look, I saw her back at the castle, after she crossed over."

"And?"

"And she was beyond the Veil, but I could still *see* her, without even trying."

Jacob frowns. "What do you think it means?"

"I don't know for sure," I admit. "But I *think* it means she's like me now." Jacob starts to protest, but I hold up my hand. "I mean, I think she has one foot on either side. I think a part of her is still tied to the Veil. I'm *hoping* that means there's a way for us to pull her back."

I don't have to read Jacob's mind to know what he's thinking. The same fear is rattling around inside my head.

What if we can't?

But he's kind enough not to say it out loud.

One step at a time, I think. First, we have to get to the graveyard.

"Into your homes!" calls a voice. I turn around to see a group of hooded figures wearing monstrous masks—birdlike faces with long beaks. They are clutching lanterns, but smoke pours out instead of light. "Guard yourselves against sickness," says one. "Be vigilant . . ."

"Aren't you a pretty thing?" coos an old woman with no teeth. She holds a bouquet of rotting flowers toward me. "Poppy for the lass. Come here, come here . . ."

I back away and nearly clip a soldier.

A bunch of them huddle against the wall, collars turned up as if against a biting wind. I can't feel a thing, but they shiver, breaths fogging the air. Their eyes slide toward me, and I murmur my apologies as Jacob and I hurry on.

If I were a good ghost hunter, I'd stop and reap these people. (Then again, if I were a good ghost hunter, I probably wouldn't be in this mess in the first place.)

I paint the map in my head to keep my nerves calm. We're almost to Greyfriars. We just have to get across the street, and down the old cobblestone road, and then—

A hand comes out of nowhere, bony, dirt-stained fingers clawing at my wrist. The hand belongs to a man in a prison cart. His face splits into a broken smile. A grimace.

"Get me out, lass."

"Let her go!" orders Jacob, pulling at the prisoner's arm.

But the grimy fingers only tighten on my skin.

"Get me out or I'll break your—"

I don't think. I bring the camera up, shoving it toward his face. His eyes cut toward the lens, and he lets go so fast that I lose my balance and stumble backward. Jacob catches me, but the camera strap comes loose and the camera itself tumbles to the cobblestones.

My whole body clenches, afraid that it will break, but it lands on its back, lens up. I duck under the prisoner's hands and crouch to grab it.

I don't mean to look at the lens.

Or rather, I don't think about *not* looking.

But the moment I see my reflection in the silvered glass, my mind goes blank, and then I'm—

In the river again, lungs filling with icy water, and this time, no one saves me.

This time, I don't come up for air.

This time, the light gets farther away and I keep sinking down, down, down until—

My vision goes black.

And it takes me a second to realize it's not an absolute darkness, but Jacob's hands over my eyes, his voice in my ear. "You're alive. You're alive. You're alive."

I shudder back to myself. I'm kneeling in the street, cobblestones digging into my shins, and chest heaving. But I'm here. Real. Alive. Or as close as I can get right now.

"Thanks," I say. My voice wavers. Jacob pretends not to notice.

"Rule number thirty-three," he says with a smile.

"Friends don't let friends get trapped in reflections?"

"That's the one."

I know he's trying to make me smile, but all that comes to mind is the horrible cold I felt, the knowledge of how that day could have ended. Should have ended. *Did* end . . . ?

"Stop," says Jacob firmly, reading my mind. "It didn't. And it won't. Not like that. Not like this. Now come on. We're almost there."

He's right.

The entrance to Greyfriars is right ahead. Around the bend, and down a sloping road. I take up the camera and loop the purple strap over my head, careful to keep the lens pointing away from me.

No wonder Jacob always averted his gaze. Never looked right into the lens.

We round the corner and start down the road. The iron of Greyfriars's gates comes into sight. And there, in front of the metal bars, a boy and a girl stand waiting.

The girl is tall and blond, in jeans and a sweatshirt and a Slytherin scarf. She looks like she could have walked straight out of the Elephant House. But the boy is from a different time. He has black hair, and sad eyes, and looks like something out of a painting, a long-ago past. They're so different, and yet they've got the same blank expressions on their faces. The same frost crawling over their skin.

My steps slow. So do Jacob's.

"Maybe they just want to talk . . ." he says.

"Maybe," I say, but I'm not feeling hopeful.

The girl straightens and stares.

The boy pushes off the iron gates and draws his hands out of his pockets, moving toward us, and I realize I've seen him before. In a yellowing photo, in the hand of an old man in a freezing house.

If you see my boy . . .

"Hi, Matthew," I say as we get closer. But he doesn't blink, doesn't seem to register the name.

Have you ever heard that saying: *There's nobody home?*

That's what it's like, the two of them staring at us with empty eyes.

"Is there some kind of password?" asks Jacob. "Like *open sesame?*"

Beyond the gates, I can hear the sound of shovels striking earth. But when I try to step around the boy, he shifts, quick as light, blocking my way.

My fingers tighten on the camera. "I'm sorry," I say, raising it in front of the boy's face. He stares vacantly into the lens.

"Watch and listen," I start.

The boy cocks his head.

"See and know."

A single slow blink.

"This is what you are."

He makes no motion as I reach into his chest, ready to take hold of his thread.

My fingers close around . . . nothing.

No ribbon. No rope.

Just empty space.

Maybe I did it wrong. Maybe—

His hand shoots out and wraps around my throat.

It happens so fast—suddenly he's shoving me back against a stone wall.

I took a self-defense course once, one of those after-school workshops that was mostly common sense (don't talk to strangers, avoid adults in vans offering candy or puppies), but toward the end, they taught us how to break free of someone's grip. Not that I can remember the instructions right now.

Luckily, I don't have to.

Jacob tackles the boy, and the two of them go down in the street.

I stagger, drawing deep lungfuls of air as the girl surges toward me. I duck under her arms and haul Jacob to his feet.

And we do the only thing we can.

We run.

CHAPTER
TWENTY-FOUR

P lan?" asks Jacob as we race down the road, past
Greyfriars.

"I'm working on it," I answer breathlessly. My camera
bobs around my neck.

It should have worked.

Why didn't it work?

"Something's wrong with them," I say.

"You mean besides the fact they're *chasing us*?" asks
Jacob.

We hit the base of the road and skid to a stop.

"Oh no."

When I was on the other side of the Veil, I could feel
the weight of it, the pressure warning me when places
were haunted, when ghosts were close. But from *this*
side, I can't feel anything.

Which is why I didn't realize *where* we were going until we're already there.

Grassmarket.

On the other side of the Veil, Grassmarket was a bustling square full of tourists and pubs, open air and history.

Here, it's still exactly what it used to be: an execution ground.

The place where hundreds of men and women met their ends.

The square is packed with ghosts, huddled around a wooden stand.

"Detour," whispers Jacob, but I can hear the boy and the girl running behind us and there's nowhere else to go, no way out but through.

I take Jacob's hand and we force our way into the dense crowd as a man is led onto the platform. A coarse rope is cinched around his neck.

I turn away, burying my face in Jacob's shoulder because there are some things you never need to see.

But the execution doesn't come.

The voices in the crowd trail off into an eerie silence. And when I look up, I see a hundred faces. The mob isn't looking at the man on the stand.

They're looking at *us*.

A woman shuffles toward me.

"The Raven came this way . . ."

A man jostles closer.

"She said she'd set us free . . ."

A child skips and twirls.

"All we had to do . . ."

An old woman grabs at my sleeve.

". . . was get ahold of *you*."

I yelp and hold up my camera like a shield, and the old woman staggers back as if struck.

Jacob takes my arm and pulls me toward the end of the square.

"We can't outrun them!" I say.

"We don't have to," he says.

And he's right. We might be stuck here in the Veil, but we're not stuck *here*, not bound to any one place, any one loop in time and memory.

All we have to do is reach the edge of Grassmarket.

Hands grab at us as we duck and twist through the crowd.

A man collars Jacob, but I twist my friend free, camera raised, and we keep running, as hard as we can. The air at the edge of Grassmarket shimmers up ahead as the mob of ghosts closes in behind and around us.

I feel fingers brush my back, trying to snag the camera strap, but the instant before they close, we veer left out of the square and onto a narrow road. Then Grassmarket vanishes behind us, like a door slamming shut.

The mob of ghosts, the hungry crowd, their cries and shouts are swallowed up by a fold in the Veil.

Jacob doubles over, gasping, and I slump against the wall, breathless and shaking. The feeling of cold is getting worse. I don't tell Jacob but he can see it on my face, read it in my panicked thoughts. My hands, when I look at them, are colorless. I'm running out of time.

I crane my head, straining to see over the rooftops until I find it. The dark gray stone of the graveyard wall.

"Come on," I say, dragging Jacob after me.

The wall flashes behind and between houses, and I keep it in my sights as we move, because the last thing I need right now, with the Raven so close and time running out, is to get *lost*.

We've carved a large circle, and we're on a narrow road that runs along the graveyard wall, almost back to the gate, when I see the boy with sad eyes—Matthew— at the mouth of the lane. A smaller child stands beside him.

Jacob skids to a stop and turns, only to find the modern-day blond girl, with two more ghosts at her back.

"Plan?" he asks again, his voice edging higher with worry.

"I'm working on it," I say, backing up until my shoulders hit the stone of the graveyard wall.

I don't know what the children want, but it doesn't involve talking.

They don't make any sound at all, not a whisper or a giggle or a grunt. You don't think about how unnerving silence is until it's everywhere.

The circle of ghosts tightens like a knot. I don't want

to find out what happens when they close the last of the gap between us.

"Stay back!" orders Jacob. When the ghosts keep coming, he shoots me a nervous look. "It was worth a try."

I press back into the wall. There's nowhere to go. We're so close. So close. I can hear the shovels hitting earth on the other side of the wall. The children close in, opening their mouths, and instead of different voices coming out, there's only one. The Raven's. Her eerie, hypnotic song pours from their lips. The notes fill the air.

Jacob's hand closes over mine.

"I'll try to distract them," he says. "You run."

"No," I say automatically, because I can't stomach the thought of going at this alone, of being stuck in the Veil or facing the Raven without my best friend. "We're in this together."

Jacob cracks a smile. "Whew," he says. "I'm glad you said that. I'm really not up for noble sacrifices. But . . ." He looks at the circle of ghosts. "What do we do now?"

I let my gaze drift up, taking in the wall. Its rough rocks, the ivy streaming down in patches, like ropes.

I have an idea.

It is, admittedly, a bad idea.

I wrap my hands around the camera. "Plan," I say firmly. "When the flash goes off, we start climbing."

Jacob groans. "I'm really not a fan of heights."

"Time to face your fear," I whisper. "Ready . . . set . . ."

I hit the button.

The camera flash goes off, and for one dazed second, the ghosts jerk backward. Their singing drops away.

In that second, we climb.

I scramble up several feet before my shoe slips. I catch myself on a weedy vine, the rocks scraping my knuckles and shins. I manage to hook my foot into the groove of a missing stone, and keep climbing up the rough wall. I don't look down, not until I reach the top.

I swing my leg over the side and glance back. Jacob is right behind me. He starts to smile, and then slips, begins to fall.

I lunge, catching his hand, and haul him up onto the stone lip beside me.

"See?" I say, breathless. "That wasn't—so hard."

Down on the street, the children stare at us, unfazed, and then start walking up the road.

"Maybe they gave up?" says Jacob hopefully.

Maybe, I think. Or maybe they're looking for another way in. Either way, I don't have time. I turn my back on them, on the rippling city, and look to the graveyard.

Greyfriars stretches out beneath us, waiting.

Church bells toll on the air, slow and sad. I scan the sloping lawn, cluttered with tombstones, trying to spot the Raven. Mist is twining through the graves, and the light is slipping low, and I can't see her from here.

I can't see her—but I know she's there.

I can feel the pull of my missing thread, as if its end were still embedded in my chest. I am a compass, and the Raven in Red is my new north.

Another shiver passes through me, a full-body wash of cold that steals the air from my lungs and leaves me struggling for balance. Jacob steadies me, and I focus on the pressure of his grip as I slowly straighten to my feet.

Jacob lets go then, preferring to stay on his hands and knees.

"It's a perfectly rational thing to be afraid of heights," he answers defensively. And far too loudly. His voice echoes through the dusk, and he clasps his hand over his mouth.

We don't have many advantages right now.

Surprise is kind of essential.

Shovels sound somewhere beyond the church, and through the fog, I can just make out a small halo of bluish light. *My* light.

It's time to get it back.

I look around and see a tall tombstone nearby, leaning up against the wall. The grave marker is a stone block with a sculpture in it, angel wings jutting out from either side and a face emerging from the stone, as if coming up for air.

I try not to look at the angel's lidded eyes or its open mouth as I shimmy down from the wall onto the nearest stone wing, then from the wing onto a single, outstretched hand.

I jump.

There's a short fall, and then my feet sink into loamy earth, thick and damp and freshly turned. Jacob lands beside me a second later and topples forward, sinking in nearly to his elbows. He groans, pulling himself free.

I get to my feet and look around, and as I do, something happens.

The Veil shimmers around us, and the graveyard shifts, the whole world blurring for one long second before stuttering back, sharp and fresh and painfully familiar. This isn't the Greyfriars I saw the other day, the one with the ghost dog running between tombstones and the man smoking at the top of the hill.

No, this is the Greyfriars of *right now*.

The Veil and the world beyond line up for the first time, two images stacked and shifted until they come into perfect focus.

The only thing that lingers is the bad feeling, like fingers down my spine.

"I don't get it," says Jacob.

But I do.

Each and every ghost creates their own Veil, paints their memory on a blank canvas. And this is *my* version.

If I fail to get my life back, if I die—*really* die—this is what my afterlife will look like. I'll be stuck wandering this graveyard, watching the Raven dig herself up, plant my life in her own bones.

But I'm not giving up.

I'm not dying here.

I'm not dying at all.

CHAPTER TWENTY-FIVE

Jacob and I snake between the graves, following the sound of shovels. We make our way up the slope and around the side of the church.

And then I see her.

The Raven in Red sits atop a large stone slab, humming softly, the glowing thread of my life tangled like a game of cat's cradle between her fingers.

She's not digging.

But I can still *hear* the shovels going. I see the glint of steel like sparks in the air, the hole growing wider at the Raven's feet like a magic trick.

And when I lift the camera to my eye and look through the viewfinder, the Veil blurs and the real world beyond comes into focus. The two places look the same, with a few *key* differences.

In the real world, the Raven still perches on the stone slab, but on that side, she's not alone. Two teenage boys stand chest-deep in the grave, obviously enchanted. Their expressions are glassy, their breaths fogging as they shovel mound after mound of dirt out of the pit and onto the grassy knoll.

I pan across the scene.

The front gates of the graveyard have been padlocked. A dull knocking sound comes from the closed doors of the church, as if someone's trapped inside. The graveyard is empty except for the Raven and the two boys.

I lower the camera, and the Veil comes back into focus. The teenagers disappear and there is only the Raven, holding my stolen life.

"Plan?" asks Jacob, and it's just bad timing, the way his voice finds the gap between shovels on dirt.

The Raven's head snaps up.

Jacob and I scramble backward, ducking behind the nearest tombstones and pressing ourselves against the broken graves.

"Sorry," he whispers.

I peer back around the corner and see the deepening hole of the Raven's grave, and suddenly, I have a plan.

It is undoubtedly a very bad plan, perhaps the worst I've ever had, and Jacob doesn't even have to ask, because he can hear me thinking it, and he's already shaking his head *no no no no no*.

But there's no time to argue.

The shovels have stopped thudding.

The Raven has stepped down from her perch.

"I need a diversion," I whisper. "Do you have my back?"

After a long moment, Jacob answers, "Always." He frowns, adding, "But if you die, I'll never forgive you."

I throw my arms around him. And then I let go. I crouch low as I half walk, half crawl between the tombstones, making a wide circle around the tree and the open pit and the Raven in Red.

The Raven walks around her grave, my life coiled in her hand. She's about to climb down into the pit when Jacob's voice rings through the graveyard.

"Hey, you!"

The Raven looks up at Jacob, who is standing on top of a tombstone.

"What's this?" she asks in that eerie, singsong way. "A little boy lost?"

"I'm not lost," he says.

She makes her way toward him, turning her back on her open grave. This is my chance. I start toward the edge of the pit as Jacob retreats, the Raven stalking him through the tombstones.

"You poor thing," she tuts. "Come to me."

The teenage boys flicker at the edge of my vision, blurred by the curtain of the Veil. They stand beside the mound of grave dirt, their eyes unfocused and their hands at their sides, still under the Raven's spell.

I'm almost to the hole when my sneakers slip. Dirt goes raining down like hail into the open grave, landing on the wooden box at the bottom. I hold my breath, but the Raven doesn't look back, and I climb down into the grave.

And onto the coffin.

I open the lid, and then, against all my better judgment, I force myself to crawl inside.

In with the bones of the Raven in Red.

Confession: Despite the bridge and the river, my worst fear has never been drowning. It's being buried alive. And as I ease the coffin lid closed, plunging myself into the dark, the air stale and close and damp, I decide that my fear hasn't changed.

I nest my body next to a skeleton in a faded red dress, pressing myself into the coffin wall. I clutch the camera and hold my breath as a weight lands on the lid.

A second later, the lid groans open.

The first thing I see is my life, raised like a lantern in the Raven's hand.

But she doesn't see me.

She is so focused on her bones that she doesn't notice me until it's too late—until she's reaching down to rest the stolen life inside her ribs and my hand shoots out and catches it first.

Heat rushes up my arm like lightning, an almost painful burst of light.

But I don't let go. I hold on for dear life, which is basically what this is.

"You stupid child," hisses the Raven.

She pulls back, trying to take the rope with her, but

252

we're connected now, by this thread between us, by my stolen life. As she straightens, she takes me with her, up out of the coffin, up to my feet, and I'm already lifting the camera with my other hand, convinced that I've done it, I've done it, I've actually beaten her—

But the Raven is too fast. Too strong.

Her free hand closes around the lens, blocking the reflection. She rips the camera from my hands, purple strap tearing as she casts it aside. The camera hits her tombstone, and I hear the horrible splinter of glass as the lens cracks, shatters, silvery shards tumbling into the grave dirt.

And before I can think, can scream, the Raven grabs me and throws me out of the grave. There's a tearing sound as I fly backward, and then I land hard on the ground. I tumble through the grass and hit a gravestone, knocking all the air out of my lungs.

A hand touches my arm and I jump, but it's just Jacob, kneeling beside me.

My camera lies broken in the dirt, but it wasn't for nothing.

Because I didn't let go.

"You are no match for me," calls the Raven.

I get to my feet. "Are you sure?" I ask, holding up the thread of life. Or at least, half of it. The end is frayed where the ribbon tore in two. The Raven looks down at her hand, where the other half glows with a diminished light, my life now divided between us. She lets out a low, inhuman snarl and lunges for me.

She's so fast, like a shadow, a bird, one moment four graves away and the next looming up right in front of me, arms spread wide like wings. But at the last instant, a figure darts between us, and all I see is the flutter of a glossy black braid before Lara lifts her mirrored pendant.

"Watch and listen!" she orders.

But the Raven cuts her gaze away in time and knocks the pendant from Lara's fingers. The necklace goes flying into the dark, and the Raven lunges for Lara.

But Lara jumps backward, narrowly escaping the Raven's talons as she tumbles into us. Jacob and I catch her.

"Sorry I'm late," she says, breathless.

"Better late than never," says Jacob.

"How did you get in?" I ask.

Lara nods at the cemetery wall. "Good thing I'm not afraid of heights. I take it," she adds, "you two have a plan."

"Of course I have a plan," I lie, shoving the glowing thread in my pocket.

The Raven starts toward us again with all the elegance of a snake.

"Well," says Lara, "just in case you *don't* have a plan, I do."

And just like that, the Raven freezes.

Not like the grieving father when he looked into my camera lens. There is no slowing, no gentle slide from movement to stillness.

No, the Raven goes rigid, arms pressed tight against her sides. She thrashes and flails, and through the gauze of the Veil, I see a man with a crown of red hair, wrapping his arms around her shoulders.

She's being pinned. By *Findley*.

"Back, ye wicked spirit!" his voice echoes through the graveyard.

I turn on Lara. "You *told* him?"

"I didn't intend to," she says, bristling. "But he followed me here, and kind of insisted."

"And he believed you?"

Lara shrugs. "We British have a high tolerance for the strange."

"Not to interrupt..." says Jacob, "but I think we have a problem."

I quickly see why.

The Raven has stopped struggling. All at once, she goes still—truly, terrifyingly still—in Findley's arms.

"Oh, children," she says, her voice slow and sickly sweet. "This just won't do."

And then she simply steps back through the Veil. Out of the world of the living, and into the land of the dead. Findley goes toppling backward, arms empty, and strikes his head on a tombstone.

But there's no time to worry about him, because the Raven is there, right in front of us, solid and bright, with those black curls and that red, red cloak.

"Your life is mine," she says. Her voice is mesmerizing, hypnotizing, but I don't let it draw me in.

"You want the rest of this thread," I say, "you've got to go through me."

"*Us,*" says Jacob.

"*All* of us," says Lara, from my other side. She's recovered her necklace, and the mirror pendant spins from her fingers.

"Is that so?" coos the Raven with a wicked smile. Her teeth are broken, sharp, and when she draws a breath to sing, I press my palms over my ears. So do Jacob and Lara.

But she's not singing for *us.*

A second later, the children come.

They stream into the graveyard, pass through the gates and around the tombstones. They rise from the ground and peer around the church.

They come from everywhere.

And they come for us.

No—for Jacob and Lara.

Because the *Raven* comes for me.

CHAPTER TWENTY-SIX

There's nowhere to run," coos the Raven.

But it doesn't stop me from trying.

I duck behind a tombstone, mind racing.

"There's nowhere to hide."

Her voice is right on top of me. Fingers curl around the top of the grave. I scramble up again, staggering backward out of reach.

"You are mine, you are mine, you are mine," she says, trailing me between the graves.

Nearby, Jacob wrestles with a pair of child ghosts as they try to pin him down. A few yards beyond him, Lara's trapped by a circle of them, her necklace useless against the hollow puppet children.

It's just me and the Raven.

One life between the two of us.

I dart between tombstones, wishing I had my camera, wishing I had anything but the frayed half of a ribbon.

And then I see it. Moonlight catches on the glassy shards at the top of the Raven's open grave.

I know what to do.

I run, as hard as I can, as fast as I can.

I can hear the Raven coming.

I can feel her at my heels.

But I don't look back.

I lunge for the pile of dirt at the edge of the grave and—

I almost make it.

Almost.

My hands sink into the fresh-turned soil as the Raven's fingers close around my ankle, hard as talons. My hand finds the edge of something sharp as she drags me back across the ground.

Pain lances through my palm but I don't let go.

Not when the Raven hauls me to my feet.

Not when she wraps a hand around my throat.

Not when she lifts me off the ground until we are face-to-face. Eye-to-eye.

"Got you," she whispers, her free hand diving into my pocket.

"Got you," I answer, holding up my prize.

A shard of the camera lens, small and silver and bright.

The edge is stained with blood where it cut my hand, but it's all I have, so I shove it into the Raven's face.

This time, she is not fast enough. This time, her hands are full—one around my throat, one fishing for my life—and she cannot let go of either, not before she sees her reflection in the glass.

"This is what you are," I say.

A gasp hisses like steam between her lips as her eyes go wide. Her face twists in fury and frustration before going vacant, smooth, like ice.

I don't know what the Raven sees in the mirror.

A mourning mother wandering the streets, calling for her missing child?

A vile woman stealing boys and girls from the safety of their homes?

I don't know who she was before she died.

I only know what she is now.

A specter made of loss and anger, fear and want.

I reach through the Raven's red cloak and into the empty hollow of her chest. The thread brushes my fingers, twitches under my hand as if it were a living thing, a snake in its cave, and I fight the urge to recoil. I swallow and take hold of the Raven's thread, and draw it out. It is heavy in my hand, and in the half-light of the graveyard, I can see that it's not a colorless ribbon, like the one I pulled from the mourning man's chest, but a *rope*.

A coil of thick black cord, made dense by dozens of thinner threads. Far more threads than should belong to a single person. Because, of course, they don't. This is why I couldn't find the thread in Matthew's chest. It wasn't there. It was *here*, each piece of the Raven's power stolen from a child.

The rope resists, but I wrap the dark cord around my fingers and *pull*.

And when the rope comes free, there is no *pop*, no *crack*, only the feeling of a great weight giving way.

The rope crumbles, dark and viscous, like mud, before dissolving into nothing.

And as soon as the rope is gone, so is the Raven.

One second she is right there, black hair curling around the hood of her red cloak, fingers knotted in my collar, and the next, she's a cloud of ash and smoke and

I'm falling through her vanished grip, back to the loamy earth.

All around the graveyard, the stolen children shudder, like candles in an open window, and then, in a single gust of wind, they simply . . . go out.

Lara slumps, breathless, against a tree, her braid half-undone.

Jacob stands atop a grave, holding a stick in both hands like a bat.

But there's no one left to fight.

Lara clears her throat. "Well, now," she says, the faintest tremble in her voice as she smooths her stained shirt. "I told you we would sort things out."

I crouch over the dark remains of the Raven, digging through the ash until I find it. The frayed ribbon of blue-white light.

The other half of my thread.

Lara sucks in a short breath at the sight of it. I don't blame her. I'm willing to bet *she's* never let a ghost steal her life, never seen her own thread outside the safety of her body, let alone torn in two.

I dig the piece from my pocket and bring the two halves together in my hands.

At first, nothing happens, and for a terrible second, I think I've ruined it, this life of mine. But Jacob rests a hand on my shoulder, and as we watch, the threads begin to weave together, mending until there's only a thin line, like a crack, where the ribbon tore.

It seems . . . fragile. Less like a lightbulb, and more like a candle, something I need to shield against the wind. But the bluish light is steady in my palm, soft and bright. The opposite of the rope I pulled from the Raven.

I bring the ribbon to my chest. I have no idea how this works, if there are words you're supposed to say, or a series of gestures, like casting a spell.

So I'm pretty relieved when the ribbon simply sinks back through my ribs, simple as a rock in the river, there, and then—

I gasp, my vision going white.

My life is—

Air in starving lungs.

A hand grabbing mine.

A light in the dark.

The pebbles beneath me on the frozen bank, and water dripping from my hair, and Jacob saying, "I've got you."

And then I'm back, not in the Veil, but in the real world, flesh and bone, shadow and light, surrounded by grass and dirt and gravestones.

I'm alive.

The air parts around Lara as she steps out of the Veil, Jacob in her wake. I want to throw my arms around them both, but Lara doesn't look like the hugging type, and Jacob and I are no longer made of the same stuff, so I settle for a grateful nod and a ghost five.

And then I see it, lying by the grave, half-buried by dirt. The broken purple strap.

The camera. It came back with me, somehow, again. When I pull it out of the dirt, I half expect to see it mended, whole, like me.

But the lens is still shattered.

My heart sinks.

Lara clears her throat. "Um, Cassidy . . ."

I follow her gaze, from the open grave to the teenage

boys staring dazedly at the shovels in their hands, to Findley on the ground, who groans and rubs his head, to the sound of sirens and the men cutting the lock on the front gate, and all I can think is:

We are in so much trouble.

PART FIVE

THAT'S A WRAP

CHAPTER
TWENTY-SEVEN

For the first time since we got to Scotland, there's not a cloud in the sky. The sun is out and the air is warm as Dad and I (and Jacob) make our way up the Royal Mile toward Bellamy's Photo Store.

It's been two days since the graveyard, and I'm officially not allowed to go anywhere without adult supervision. Mom and Dad look at me like I might slip away at any second, vanish right before their eyes.

Trouble, it turned out, was kind of an understatement.

My parents had to come and get me from the police station. They walked in to find me with Findley on one side and Lara on the other (and Jacob, though it turns out you can get away with a lot when no one can see you), all of us dazed and covered in grave dirt.

Needless to say, there was a scene. A minor vandalism charge, though luckily I wasn't the one who desecrated a grave. At least, not directly. The teenage boys claimed they didn't remember anything, and even though I knew they were telling the truth, the cops still wrote them up. I felt bad for them, but they're pretty lucky to be alive.

And I was in plenty of trouble myself.

Apparently Lara had told my parents that I'd explain *everything* when I got back. Only, I couldn't. I couldn't explain where I'd gone or what had happened to me. I couldn't explain *anything*—well, I *could*, but it was the kind of explanation that led to more questions than answers.

It didn't stop me from *trying* to tell them the truth.

"Ten points for story," said Mom when I was done, but Dad still grounded me for life. In the end, I think they were just really scared, and really glad I was alive.

So was I.

Filming for the first episode of *The Inspecters* finished yesterday. Mom's back at the flat packing up and looking through the footage with the crew. It took an hour of begging for Dad to take me to Bellamy's, and in the end, I think he only said yes because the weather's so nice and he wanted an excuse to go out.

My camera may be broken, but its back stayed on. There's still film inside. And I want to see what it saw.

Dad and I reach the top of the road and turn to look back down the Royal Mile, the street rolling away like a ribbon down the hill.

"It's quite a city," Dad says.

"Yeah," I say. "It really is."

Bellamy's is open but empty. No customers. No one behind the counter. Jacob and Dad stay outside while I head in. It feels strange, coming here. I miss my dark-room, and I feel weird leaving the photos with someone else. Weird not being the first one to see how they turn out, to watch the pictures rise up through the pool of developer. But I don't have much choice.

"Hello?" I call.

I hear a shuffle, and then a second later a girl pops out from a room in the back. She's older than me, but not as

271

old as I expect, maybe eighteen, with short blue hair and rainbow nails.

"Hiya!" she says with a strong Scottish lilt.

"I was wondering if you develop black-and-white film?" I ask.

"Wouldn't be much of a photo shop if we didn't! Truth be told," she says, leaning her elbows on the counter, "it's my favorite kind. There's just something about that old film—the world looks different in black-and-white. Stranger. More magical. You know what I mean?" Her eyes go to the camera in my hands. "Goodness, what have you been doing, playing football with it?"

I set the battered camera on the counter.

"I know it's broken," I say, "but there's film in there, and I was hoping . . ."

She pokes it with a nail. "Can I?" she asks, already taking it up. She handles the camera gingerly, lovingly, as she turns it over. "This is an old model, hard to match."

"Match?"

"Aye, it's just a broken lens. Well, and a cracked

viewfinder. I can't help you there, but . . ." With a deft motion and a soft click, the ruined lens comes free in her hand. "Some silvering on the glass . . . hmmm . . ." She vanishes into the back and returns a few minutes later with a new lens. Well, not a *new* one. It's clearly as old as the camera. With a quick turn, she attaches it. "There we are."

My heart soars at the sight of the mended camera, then sinks. "I can't afford—"

She sets the camera on the counter. "Can't sell this lens, actually." She turns it toward me, and for a second, I flinch, remembering the mirrored surface, the memory, but when I look at the lens, I just see me. Or at least, mostly me. For a moment, it looks like my hair is floating, and a light hovers over my chest. But it could just be a lens flare, a trick of the eye, because when I blink, it's gone.

"See?" she says, tapping the lens. "It's got a defect. Right there." I squint and see a small smudge, like a cloud of fog, on the inside of the glass. "Makes pictures come out a little funny. You'd be taking it off my hands."

I bite my lip. "Are you sure?"

"Aye!" she says, taking up the camera. "I'll get this film sorted for you and—oh, you've got one left, did you know?" She wiggles the camera. "Want me to take it?"

I glance around, suddenly uncomfortable at the idea of being *in* the shot instead of taking it. And then I spot Jacob through the front window. He's got his back to me as he watches people pass.

"Hold on a sec," I say.

I go to the window and lean my back against the pane so that Jacob and I are side by side, with only the glass and the curling script of BELLAMY's between us.

He sees me, glances back over his shoulder, smiles. I smile back, and I hear the soft click of the camera as the shop girl takes the shot.

"Nice light this time of day," she says, winding the film. "That should turn out well."

"Thanks," I say, returning to the counter. "I hope so."

She pops the back of the camera open and plucks out the canister. My fingers tickle and I have to fight back the urge to reach for it. Instead, I watch it disappear into an envelope.

"Come back tomorrow morning," she says. "I'll have it ready for you."

Back at the Lane's End that night, we order fish and chips and gather around—the crew, Mom and Dad, Findley, Jacob, and me—to watch a rough cut of the footage from *The Inspecters* "Episode 1: City of Ghosts." I wish Lara were here, too, but I haven't seen her since the night of the Greyfriars incident. (I'm pretty sure Mrs. Weathershire thinks I'm a bad influence.)

Jacob and I sit side by side on the sofa, my arm against his, while on the TV screen, Dad recounts the history of Mary King's Close. Mom offers notes on where to cut, and scribbles down lines they might want to add in voiceover. Grim sits on Findley's lap, despite the fact Findley bellows with laughter whenever anyone jumps on camera—he calls it "catching fright."

Findley claims he doesn't remember anything about that night in the graveyard, but there's a bruise on his cheek, half-hidden by the scruff of his beard, and a glint in his eye whenever it catches mine.

On the screen, Mom's voice echoes through the prison cells at the castle.

It feels so long ago, so far away. I guess in some ways it is.

When it's time for everyone to leave, Findley wraps me in a bear hug.

"Thank you," I whisper, "for everything."

"There's a mark on you, Cassidy," he says, suddenly sober. "You be careful now."

Tears prick my eyes. I'm not sure why.

But it's still hard to let go.

The next morning, it takes half an hour to catch Grim, who's decided, in a rare burst of *basic feline dignity*, that he is never going back in his crate.

"Come on, kitty," says Jacob, trying to scare him out from under the sofa. I take the approach of making a trail of cat treats across the room.

While Jacob and I wrangle Grim, Mom and Dad

finish packing, and for a little while everything feels normal. The air is buzzing with excitement and nervous energy, all of us ready to put this city behind us, albeit for different reasons.

Finally, Jacob and I slump onto the sofa with a crated Grim between us.

"Did he scratch you?" asks Mom, coming into the room.

I frown, confused. "No, why?"

"Your palm."

I look down. She's right. Not about Grim, but about my hand.

I rub my thumb over the shallow red line, the place where the lens shard sliced me in the graveyard. There's no *cut*, but it still aches.

"No," I say, "I'm fine."

When it's time to go, we drag our bags downstairs, where Mrs. Weathershire is waiting.

"Off, then?" she asks cheerfully. "I'll phone a cab."

Mom and Dad head out to the curb. I'm right behind them, but I stop and turn around when footsteps sound on the stairs. It's not the ghostly Mr. Weathershire this time. It's Lara. She pulls up, breathless, as if afraid she was going to miss me. A few flyaway hairs escape her braid. She smooths them down.

"Hey!" I say, glad to see her.

"Hey," she says, shooting Jacob a measuring look before turning back to me.

"How do you feel?"

"Like my life's been torn in two," I say dryly.

Her eyes widen. "Really?"

I shake my head and laugh. "I feel fine. Normal. Well, as normal as it gets. Are you in much trouble?"

Lara shrugs. "Nothing I can't handle." I'm surprised to see a glimmer in her eye, something close to mischief. "It might surprise you to know that I have, on occasion, broken a *few* rules."

She takes one of my bags, following me out to the curb. "We need to talk."

Jacob hovers.

Give us a second, I think, and he frowns but shuffles away.

Lara waits until he's gone. "You're not doing him a favor," she says, "keeping him here."

Not this again. "He's my best friend, Lara."

"That may be, but there's a difference between wanting to stay and being too afraid to let go. You need to send him on."

I turn to her. "You didn't send your uncle on."

Lara stills. *"What?"*

"I met him, when I was looking for you. He's the one who taught you, isn't he? About ghosts and in-betweeners. About the Veil and mirrors and the deals we made and what we're supposed to do. You said you learned from his library, but that's not exactly true, is it?"

Lara hesitates, then shakes her head. "He didn't start teaching me until after . . ."

She trails off, and I don't know if she means after he died, or *she* did.

"You knew he was here," I say, "at the Lane's End. You knew what he was, and what you were, but you didn't send him on."

"He's not like the others," she says defensively.

"I know," I shoot back, "and neither is Jacob."

Lara crosses her arms. "You're right. I didn't send Uncle Reggie on, but I didn't pull him across the Veil, either." She steps closer, lowering her voice. "Jacob used you to cross over, and you're anchoring him here, and the longer he stays, the stronger he'll get. He's dangerous, Cassidy."

We both turn to look at Jacob, who's now stalking a flock of pigeons, trying to spook them into flight.

"I'll take my chances," I say.

Lara sighs. "All right. Just be careful." She turns to go, then doubles back. "Oh, before I forget..." She draws her mirror pendant over her head. "Here," she says, offering it to me.

I'm already reaching for it when I force myself to stop.

"I can't take that," I say. "You need it."

"Don't worry," she says, pulling a second one from her pocket. "I always keep a spare."

When I still don't take the necklace, she steps closer and loops the cord over my head.

"Thank you," I say, tucking the cool disk under my shirt. "For everything."

Lara shrugs, as if it's nothing, but we both know better. We're bound by more than matching pendants.

Our cab pulls up to the curb. Lara hands me a slip of paper.

"My email," says Lara. "In case you find yourself in trouble again."

"Oh," I say, "I doubt that will happen."

Lara actually snorts, an almost indelicate sound. Then she pokes me in the chest. "Be careful with that."

"I will," I say, fingers drifting to the pendant.

She shakes her head. "I wasn't talking about the necklace."

With that, Lara spins on her heel and marches back up the front steps.

"Bye, Lara!" calls Jacob.

She looks back over her shoulder. "Bye, ghost," she says.

And then she slips inside.

Grim sits on the seat beside me, emitting a low growl from within his crate. Jacob stares out the window as the city slides past, the castle looming in the distance.

Mom and Dad are already looking through their next folder, talking about stories and scripts as we head for a new city, a new film crew, a new guide.

A new episode.

A new chapter.

But there's one last stop before we go.

* * *

The girl behind the counter at Bellamy's smiles when she sees me.

Mom and Dad stay in the cab, which I guess is a sign of progress, though I know it'll be a while before I've earned their trust again.

The shop girl ducks into the back and returns with an envelope. She whistles as she sets it on the counter. "Some of these are crazy."

"You looked?"

"Sorry." She shrugs. "Part of the job. But you've got skills. Most people couldn't pull off these kinds of tricks without digital editing." She taps a rainbow nail on the envelope. "You really captured this city," she says, handing me the pictures. I thank her and accept them, paying her with the money Dad gave me in the car.

"The last photo is my favorite," she adds with a wink.

I don't look until I'm back in the car.

The envelope is covered in touristy photos, random couples posing in front of famous buildings, sharing meals on rooftops, standing on mountains.

Other people go on trips and take pictures of buildings.

I go on trips and take pictures of ghosts.

I draw the stack of photos out.

There's one of the Lane's End: Mrs. Weathershire in the doorway with a tray of tea.

Next, the Royal Mile, with its street performers and bustling crowds.

And Greyfriars, once, dotted with tourists. And a second time, grayer, with wisps of fog.

There's Mary King's Close, with its high walls and its uneven light, the shadow of something strange peering out of the dark.

My parents and Findley standing beneath streetlamps at night, and Lara standing on the stairs. The mournful father in his winter house, and the castle with its portcullis and its cannons and its prison cells.

Things get strange after that. In the Veil. A dozen photos, and almost nothing came out. Streaks and smudges that could be faces, hands, or just a trick of the light.

If you didn't know, you might think the film was exposed the wrong way.

But I know. I can see the ghosts in the shades of gray.

And there, at the end, the last photo. The only one *I* didn't take.

In it, I'm leaning up against the photo store window. On the other side of the glass is a smudge, a wisp of smoke in the shape of a boy. It could be a weird reflection, some distortion, but it's not.

I see the telltale flop of his hair. The curve of his mouth. The turn of his head as he glances back. The edge of a smile.

There's a difference between wanting to stay and being too afraid to let go.

In the cab, Jacob looks over at me, like he can read my mind. Of course, he can.

"When I saved you from the river," he says, "you saved me from something, too." I hold my breath. It's the first time Jacob's ever talked about his life—or death—before we met. I want him to go on, but of course, he doesn't.

He holds up his hand, as if waiting for a ghost five, but this time, when we bring our palms together, we don't make a smacking sound. We don't pull away. We let them stay. And I swear I can almost feel his touch.

The longer he stays, the stronger he'll get.

But then it's gone.

The car slows to a stop outside the airport.

Mom and Dad pay the cab driver, and then we all pile out: two parents, a girl, a ghost, and a ticked-off cat, ready for the next adventure.

ACKNOWLEDGMENTS

This book is dedicated to several people, and a very old city. The city, I've already thanked. The people, only a few of whom I'll remember to name:

To my mum, who always encouraged me to get lost on purpose, and my dad, who always helped me find my way back when I did.

To my agent, Holly, and my editor, Aimee, for always being up for an adventure, even when they didn't know where it would lead.

To Cat, Caro, and Ciara, for being the best part about this city, and Dhonielle, and Zoraida, for keeping me company on this long, winding road.

To the team at Scholastic, for letting me write this sometimes scary, always strange, little book.

ABOUT THE AUTHOR

Victoria (V. E.) Schwab is the #1 *New York Times*–bestselling author of more than a dozen novels for young adults and adults, including the Shades of Magic series, *Vicious*, *Vengeful*, *This Savage Song*, and *Our Dark Duet*. Victoria lives in Nashville, Tennessee, but she can often be found haunting Paris streets and trudging up Scottish hillsides. Usually, she's tucked in the corner of a coffee shop, dreaming up stories. Visit her online at veschwab.com.